CHOOSING LIFE:
A PRO-LIFE ANTHOLOGY

CHOOSING LIFE:
A Pro-Life Anthology

ISBN: 979-8-9948030-0-4

This anthology contains several works of fiction. Names, characters, and incidents are all products of the different authors' imaginations or are used for fictional purposes. Any resemblance to actual events or persons, living or dead, is entirely coincidental. Any mentions of name brands, places, and trademarks remain the property of their respective owners, bear no association with the authors or the publisher, and are used for fictional purposes only.

Cover Illustration and typesetting by Christopher Jackson

Cover design by Allen Steadham and Christopher Jackson

Edited by Allen Steadham

INTRODUCTION BY ALLEN STEADHAM

In 2023, after I finished heading the *Christmas Miracles* anthology project, I had inspiration from the Lord to put together a pro-life anthology. Almost a year later, I started reaching out to fellow Christian fiction authors I'd worked with on other anthology projects: H.A. Pruitt, Parker J. Cole, Joanna White, and Lauren Smyth. Thankfully, they accepted my invitation, and this project came together beautifully. Each offered their own perspectives in their signature styles.

My own 2019 debut novel *Mindfire* was a pro-life Christian fiction superhero story. Even before I became a Christian, I took a pro-life stance in the early 1990s when a close friend faced a difficult choice over an unplanned pregnancy and whether she could handle life as a single mother. We spoke at length about it, and I did my best to encourage her to keep the baby. Ultimately, she chose to have that child and raised him to adulthood. She never regretted her decision.

When I gave my life to Christ, things became even clearer to me. Each child is precious in God's sight regardless of circumstance, ability, or any other factor. And each child has tremendous potential that only God knows. Being pro-life doesn't mean ignoring any traumas the mother has gone through, and it doesn't excuse any misdeeds done to the mother; it simply acknowledges that the growing life inside her has done nothing wrong and deserves the chance to be born. There are options such as foster care and adoption available if the mother can't raise her child.

Many people make the argument that a child isn't "alive" until it is born or is viable. They call the embryo or fetus a "clump of cells" — as if cells aren't alive or part of the life cycle. Life begins at conception, initiating a nine-month biological process that results from a baby's creation. Abortion doesn't just stop a pregnancy from being completed; it ends the baby's (or babies') life (lives), whatever stage of development they are at. Therefore, abortion is murder. If the baby was not alive, they would not have to be killed. Whether by surgical procedure or the taking of pills, the baby's heartbeat stops, and their life ends in terrible, traumatizing pain.

Many mothers who chose abortion later report regretting their decision. Statistically, one-third of women who undergo abortions go through post-natal depression and are more likely to engage in self-harming behaviors. Men who wished to become fathers but either didn't know their partner or spouse had an abortion or were unable to persuade them from having an abortion are traumatized as well. Everyone involved loses something.

Some make the argument that the pro-life movement is only "pro-birth." That is not true. Many people who are involved with the movement want to see women receive support throughout and beyond their pregnancies. Many pro-life organizations make this a part of their missions. Life goes far beyond birth.

Each of the stories in this anthology concerns unplanned pregnancies and each have resolutions where the mother chooses life. But these aren't superficial or cut-and-dry fiction. They acknowledge each woman's individual challenges, worries, and lifestyles. They're heartfelt and powerful tales that address the tough questions surrounding unplanned or even unwelcome pregnancies and abortion. It is our hope that these stories make the reader think about this important issue and consider that abortion is never "necessary." There are always alternatives.

And they all involve Choosing Life.

I hope you enjoy this anthology.

Sincerely,

Allen Steadham (author of "1:30 P.M.")

Dedicated to the memory of Charlie Kirk and his trailblazing work in pro-life advocacy.

IRIS

By H.A. PRUITT

"Mamaaa!"

Oh, Lord, please.

"I need go potty!"

God, please, I just need a minute.

"Mom, baby...baby James...baby James is eating the carpet!"

My two older boys continue shouting and banging on the bedroom door. In the connected bathroom, I relent and shove the test in a diaper in the little trash bin that we keep in the bathtub, so James doesn't dig through it. I'll take it to the porch trash can before my husband comes home from the office. It's Tuesday, so I could take the bag to the street dumpster and watch the trash truck carry it away all before noon.

I stand and catch my reflection in the mirror. I'm surprised my round face still looks fairly young and rosy and that my long brown hair isn't frizzled like a rat's nest but laying in limp waves. I feel like I ought to look much older and haggard.

"Mamaaa!"

"Stop yelling in the house!" I yell while throwing my hair up into a tight bun and storming through the bathroom then the bedroom to the door. I shouldn't be this frustrated this early, but now I know why I've been more irritable lately, and I relish having an excuse.

But I don't want the excuse to be true.

The little plus sign I stared at for too long stirs up my nausea, and I breathe in the peppermint oil I dabbed on my wrist while waiting on the pregnancy test.

Then I open the door.

Eli, my toddler, stops screaming. He bolts to the sink in our master bathroom, his thick, unruly brown hair flopping like a cockatoo's crest. "I need low-tin!" he shrills as he hops in his mini training potty and snatches the soap pump bottle off the counter. Before I can correct or stop him, Richard calls from the doorway.

"I gave James some grapes so he'd stop eating—"

"No!" I shoot past him and run through half of our one-story farmhouse before finding my blue-eyed eleven-month-old standing before a wide-open fridge. He's clutching a grape in each hand, one is sticking out of his mouth, and an upended bowl of cereal sits between his feet. He plops on his bottom, and the sickening *crunch* of a new mess to clean up nearly makes me vomit. James's little cheeks turn red, and he grunts.

"Please don't poop. Not right n—"

A crash resounds from the bathroom.

"Aunt Iris, Eli broke something!" Richard reports to me, grinning like a red-headed leprechaun at all the havoc.

Eli's shriek breaks loose.

James starts screaming.

God, I don't want to be pregnant again.

•••

Seven chaotic, loud, overwhelming hours later, Eli is napping in his toddler bed, James is quietly harassing an empty milk jug, and Richard is at first grade.

God, thank you for school. And nap time.

Knowing I may only have minutes before James decides he wants to start screaming for no reason, I check the notifications on my phone. I scan the long list I've been forced to ignore all day while cleaning up a never-ending cycle of poop, milk, snot, toys, school papers, and random socks. No part of me wants to open any of my emails. I'm juggling four clients for my freelance graphic design business, but as with my two previous pregnancies, my creativity has tanked, I'm exhausted, and I'm even more of a cranky introvert than usual. A text from William, my husband, catches my attention, and I open it.

We have the last papers to sign to finalize everything for Richard.

Good, I text back then thank God that the awful stint of foster care will soon end for good. The caseworkers often told Richard too much or promised him empty words and brought him more instability than healing. Their constant visits also had reminded him that he wasn't really part of our family. But in the month since we took him to court to make him our son forever, Richard's calm and sense of belonging have blossomed and taken root. His violent weekly blow-ups ended. And, even though it can manifest as bossiness and snitching on Eli, his helpful side has brightened.

William and I have always been glad we could step in for Richard, but dealing with the system and all the ways it left us and him in limbo has caused us all grief and stress nearly every day for the past ...

I squint at the calendar I designed. The top has a scrapbook-like collage of pictures from last January: Eli in the kitchen on the antique tricycle William restored for him, Richard grinning with his red hair falling in his eyes and a kindergarten drawing in his hands, and an action shot of Chartreuse the guinea pig running from Eli. I smile, but it fades as my gaze lands on the date. Today is January 14, 2025. Although I'm staring at the proof, I can't believe we've been dealing with the foster care mess for nearly five years.

William and I never signed up for foster care. A terrible situation in his family had forced Richard and his five brothers and sisters into our home. In one hour, we had changed from two married people to parents with six kids who didn't want us to be their parents. Every day had become a nightmare of dealing with the sickening reality of what had necessitated, they instantly leave their home while trying not to drown in the madness of six kids who lacked love and life skills and who demanded attention in all the worst ways. As time passed, some had to go to special facilities, and other homes that actually signed up for foster care had opened for the rest of Richard's siblings, but none wanted him.

I had been pregnant or nursing a newborn most of that time—first Eli and then James—and the rollercoaster of raging hormones, incapacitating sickness, and confusing tangle of grief over losing children who never were mine yet had become mine had left me with a complex, deep-seated reluctance to have another child or pregnancy.

Oh, God, let that test be wrong.

I take a deep breath. The nausea and dizziness tell me the positive test hasn't lied.

I can't, I beg God. *I can't be pregnant again. I can't handle another kid. These three are absolute chaos. And Richard—he needs so, so much attention, and he just got out of that family with so many brothers and sisters. He finally doesn't feel neglected. And I can't be sick like this when I need to take care of little James. And how am I supposed to keep up with Eli? I can't even do that now. And I am getting closer to thirty-five. Everyone says that's when you need to stop having kids for their health and yours. William's knees are getting close to forty. He can still chase Eli and play on the floor, but I don't know how much longer—*

A slow rip pulls me out of the prayer.

I find James biting a page out of his daddy's commentary of James.

As I rescue the remnants and shove the book back on the shelf, I tell God, *I can't even handle one. Please don't let us have a fourth.*

•••

The next day, James refuses to take a nap. He usually fights sleep like it's his fiercest enemy, but after a morning of Eli dumping every toy bin he owns, refusing to pick up any of it, and spitting on me when I put him in time out, James is kicking my last nerve.

I strap him into the baby carrier and walk while I try to read my design clients' emails, but he repeatedly flings his head back until he bashes my phone out of my hand. It lands on the kitchen linoleum, screen side down. I stare at the purple case, dreading what I'll find if I flip it over. The thought of losing all my designs and all my personal artwork saved on it pushes up the compulsion to scream at James. I unbuckle the carrier as fast as I can and set James on the floor so he can scream at me instead. He howls and falls backward on the floor then rolls on his side and pulls my phone into his clutches.

"I don't care! Cry!" I snap then rip the phone out of his hands. My rage instantly flips to guilt, and the next second, I'm crying on the floor rocking him, he's pulling hair out of my bun, and I'm praying.

See, God? See? I can't handle this. I don't want to be this mean pregnant lady. I don't want to lose my temper with James. But, God, these pregnancy hormones! I feel like I can't control myself. I feel like some evil alien has taken over my body, and I don't know where in outer space the real me got dumped. I've been someone else for nearly four years now. I don't want to get even more lost in this cycle of pregnancy, postpartum, and being a mom without a break. I want to get back to living and not just existing as a twenty-four-hour vending machine that shoots out whatever everyone else needs without ever having a break or time to look for myself out there in outer space. Am I even out there somewhere anymore? Oh, God, please, I need to not be pregnant. I need this to not be real, to go away, to—

"Mama!" Eli bangs on his bedroom door. I check my thankfully intact phone screen. We've woken him up after only thirty-five minutes. He usually sleeps two or three hours.

I cry harder, knowing Eli will be overtired and thus a ball of obstinate, cranky energy for the rest of the day.

•••

We survive Eli's surly mood by playing with his multitude of toy vehicles. Besides pushing James away from his favorite tractors, Eli stays calm, and I start to feel glad to putter around with them. But four o'clock announces itself as the school bus honking from the road.

I stand and stumble through the awful mess of trucks, excavators, tractors, and cars.

The bus honks more insistently.

"Okay, okay, okay!" I tear open the door and wave. James tries to escape onto the porch, but I catch him then peer around the yard for Richard.

He is slothfully tottering down the driveway.

The bus honks again.

"Come on, Richard!" I shout so the bus driver will notice me and stop harassing me.

Something knocks my leg, and Eli darts across the ice-slush covered porch and down the ramp in nothing but his training pants and cowboy hat.

"Rich—E—gah!" I sputter and shriek. "Get back here right now!"

James yowls and grabs my hopelessly disheveled bun. After ripping my hair from his fingers, I plop him inside, slam the door despite his screaming protests, and sprint after Eli. The short, often interrupted jog I get most mornings must be keeping my legs in shape because I catch him before he reaches the road.

Richard stops his scant progress. "Aunt Iris ... Are we ... Aunt Iris, are we ... Are we going to play ...?"

I want to scream at him to just spit out what he wants to say.

"Aunt Iris, are we playing outside?" Richard drops his backpack in the half ice, half mud driveway.

"Rich—aahd!" Eli bites my arm in an attempt to escape, and I sling him into a football hold.

"Inside," I seethe through gritted teeth. "Get your backpack and get inside."

"Ow-side! Ow-side! I wantta play ow-side!" Eli shrills, flailing all his limbs. His hat flies off. "No! Hat! My haaat!"

Thankfully, Richard complies even though he starts incessantly chattering, and I pick up Eli's hat and follow him.

Once we finally make it inside, I head to the kitchen to make dinner. James follows me, wailing, and I try to hold him while finding something simple to make, but he keeps pulling my hair, and I have to put him down to keep from exploding.

Because I'm too exhausted to cook anything, too tired to fight to get the boys to eat but also feeling too much degrading guilt about my un-mom-like behavior to give them junk, I open a can of peas and slap some natural peanut butter on wheat bread. James clings to my legs while whine-screaming the whole time, so it takes longer than it should.

When I call them to the table, Eli scurries to the living room and dives under the pile of cushions he's pulled off the couch. As I try to wrestle him out, Richard starts telling me a story, James falls on the linoleum and starts raging, and our two guinea pigs begin wheeking. The cacophony of rackets assaults my head like knives stabbing my eyeballs and grating across my teeth.

"Be quiet! Everybody be quiet!" I cry then start weeping.

Richard keeps talking.

Eli slaps my face.

James pulls my sweatpants down enough that I release Eli, and he dashes into his room and slams the door.

"Why?! Why is it so hard to just go to the table and *eat food?!*" I scream. "Why?!"

Richard apparently realizes I'm upset and scampers to the table. I yank James off me and carry him to his highchair. After buckling him in and giving him his sippy cup, I go after Eli. I find him in his toy box, throwing out all the toys.

"I take bath."

"No, it's time for dinner."

"No! I wantta bath! I wantta baaath!" He hurls a toy keyboard at me. The kid has excellent aim and pegs my shin.

"Guh—E—argh!" I shriek, my brain too overwhelmed to form words. "Absolutely not! Absolutely *not!*"

"Asbo-lut-lee not!" he mimics me, pointing and squishing his strong yet narrow features into the meanest face he can.

"Stop!" I head for him.

He shrills, hops out of the toy box, and runs to the kitchen.

By the time I reach him, he has buckled his booster seat and William is striding in the door.

The scents of leather, onion and pepper burrito, and coffee jump off him and smack me in the stomach. My nausea spikes into my throat, and I rush into the master bathroom without even giving him a smile.

I reach the wall by the toilet and drop onto the bathroom floor. I feel awful. I'm about to throw up, my emotions are flailing, and I've been a jerk to everyone all day. Yet I can't stop thinking how much I want to scream at everyone to shut up and leave me alone.

I hate this. I can't be pregnant. I hate this! I hate being so mean and out of control! I don't like being like this! Who am I anymore? I used to be so fun and happy, and I was never an angry or mean person, but these kids—these hormones, being pregnant, having to keep on my mom face every single stupid second of the day—I'm somebody else. Who am I? Who am I?!"

"Iris?"

I don't answer, but William finds me. He sits on the floor, his broad shoulders taking up the rest of the space between the toilet and shower, and hugs me. "Hard day?"

I nod against his thick, dark beard. His big, warm arms wrapped around my little frame calm me enough to still my tears. I curl against him, wishing we had more time together. We hardly have a minute not taken up by work, church, or the kids.

Am I even the person he married anymore? Or am I all gone? Is having kids taking us away from each other? It feels like it. It so, so feels like it. Am I just empty? Nothing? Like a shell that is full of a ghost of a person trying to be a mom yet only being an evil, screaming failure at life?

"I'm sorry they were trolls," he murmurs as waves of Richard's signature maniacal laughter float from the kitchen. "They're a lot."

He smells so strongly of coffee, which to my nose smells like the sourest cigarettes mixed with the most bitter skunk spray, that I can't open my mouth to answer. I just nod again.

"Stay in here until it's time for church," he tells me. "I'll handle the boys. Have you eaten?"

After I shake my head, we separate.

"What can I get you?" he asks as he stands and starts wandering around our connected master bathroom and bedroom.

"Um, I don't know. A peanut butter sandwich and some berries." Though the thought of food disgusts me, I need William to believe my despair is stemming from nothing more than a hard day. I can't let him know the truth because then ...

"Have you seen my house shoes?" He looks in our closet.

"I think one is in Eli's potty, which is in the tub."

"Of course it is. James is in full kleptomaniac mode." He retrieves it out of the mini potty and examines it. "Phew, it's dry."

"I still haven't found my purple hair tie." I sigh.

"Little kleptos," he laughs, looking in the cotton ball drawer and finding a toy car. "At least they pay for what they pilfer."

"Oh, your other shoe is in the dirty clothes basket." I point where I just spotted it. I push up off the floor and trail away from the stinking toilet to the sink that still smells like the peppermint oil Eli dumped when he was supposed to be on his potty earlier.

William grabs his second shoe and shoves his foot in it as stampeding feet echo through the house.

I drop my face on my palm. "They are *supposed* to be eating *at the table,"* I growl. "They have been such jerks today!" *Or have they? Is it just me overreacting to everything and being the jerk?*

"Uh—"

I look up.

William dumps a cache of Goldfish crackers out of his shoe. "Eli has paid in gold."

"I'm sorry," I groan. "I don't even know how he got in here with those—"

"Dada! Dada! Dada!" Eli shrills and bangs on the door. "I want Dadaaa!"

Tears burst out of me. "Make him go away. Please make him go away! Make them go away!"

"Hey, breathe. Breathe," William soothingly says. "James' check-up is tomorrow. I'll take both the little ones, and we'll see Grandma and get lunch. Maybe go by Tractor Supply and pretend to ride the four wheelers."

"No, I didn't mean—I don't want you to have to take off work all day."

"I can, and you need some time." He hooks on his house shoe then gives me another hug. "It's okay."

A wild squeal belts out from the kitchen.

"It will be okay," he amends. "It will."

"Okay." I know it isn't okay and that it won't be okay for a long time, but I need to pretend that the pregnancy isn't real because he wants a girl so desperately. He has said it would be wonderful to have a little Iris to love. He takes such attentive care of me, and I know he would be the sweetest girl dad. But I know that another me or another child that comes in any form would steal away any of my self and breathing room that might be left.

I can't do this, I tell God, but I tell William, "Yeah. Thanks. I do just need a break. They are a lot."

He eyes me like he knows I'm withholding something, but the clear sound of James' cup crashing to the floor turns both our faces to the door. William heads into the mayhem of the boys, and I pray, *God, please make a way for this to not happen."*

•••

On the way to Wednesday night Bible study, Richard interrupts every attempt William and I make to talk to each other in the van. Being the pastor and pastor's wife, we arrive early to set up. Once inside, though, James attacks the trash can, and while we're cleaning it up, Eli finds a box of little offering envelopes and throws them everywhere, yelling, "It snowing! It snowing!"

We're both frustrated by the time other people start arriving, but the presence of our close-knit church family diffuses our tension and their chaotic energy. James hushes and clings to my neck while eyeing everyone, and the older boys flit around, earning adoration from the small crowd, until William says it's time to start. Then the three boys go to their class, which only includes them and one other toddler, and we settle down in our adult class.

An older woman teaches, and I try to pay attention. The church building is small, though, and James' screaming nearly drowns out our class discussion. My mom brain can't help but debate itself about whether I should go get him or not. I also wonder if the other two are being good for their teacher since I can hear Richard talking non-stop and way too loudly.

Eventually, I do go get James and take him to the nursery. He fights for a few minutes but sleep wins.

I decide to sit in the glider chair rather than return to class and risk waking him up. As I rock him, I stare at the wall art I made when we first set up the nursery before we had the foster kids. It hangs over the crib and says, "God made me wonderful."

They are wonderful, God. I know that. Not every day is like this one and yesterday, and I know James is probably screaming incessantly because he's teething. And that will end at some point. But I'm so tired of missing church because of them. I'm so tired of feeling distant from you because of them. I can't pray or read my Bible without being interrupted a million times, and I hate that it's so hard to retain anything I do get to read because my brain is so full of all the things I have to do, all the stuff going on, and all the noise in the house. God, I'm sorry I'm struggling, but I ... What am I supposed to do? Even on good days, I still have to feed them, and change diapers, and stop them from climbing the bookshelves or locking each other in the dryer. It never ends. I even dream about them! That one where James was a monster baby that wouldn't stop chasing me while screaming like a siren was awful. And that one of Eli dying was—no. I hate the crazy, paranoid mom and pregnancy dreams. Being a mom never, never stops. It's so hard. They are so much. So, so much. And they take so much out of me. I feel like I'm a worse mom with more kids. I feel like I'm a worse wife with more kids. I feel like I'm ... nothing. I'm just a mom. That's it. Nothing else. Not myself, not William's wife, not even yours, God. Please, I don't want to fall deeper in this dark pit of being nothing but a mom and not knowing who I am, or how to get back to who I was before kids, or even if I want to go back, or if I'm better or worse, or... Please. Not another one. Just don't let it be real. I pray that last plea over and over until someone knocks softly on the nursery door.

William pokes his head in. "Is he asleep?"

I nod.

"Okay, stay here, and I'll get you two after I load up the boys." William hates the baby rage screams as much as I hate the hair pulling and will do anything to avoid them. I'm thankful for him doing what I see as the more difficult task, though. Nearly every time we load up after everyone else leaves, Eli escapes the church and runs around the lawn laughing until one of us catches him, and Richard has a special talent of being so slow, Eli escapes three more times before Richard even makes it to the van.

I hear Eli and William yelling, and I know the typical chase has ensued. They are both so strong-willed that they constantly drive one another into fits, but they are also so alike in their love for others that they never stay mad for more than a few minutes.

"Come on, Richard!" William shouts.

Oh, Lord, that kid is so slow. Please help William get both of them in the van so we can go home.

I close my eyes and try to relax. I'm so tired, and from the sounds coming from them, we still have a battle ahead before all the boys are even buckled in.

•••

I carry James from the pediatric waiting room to the OBGYN reception desk. Although William had promised to give me a break and he usually takes the kids to their appointments, our third family flu this winter snuck up on him through the night, and he was happy to let me take James to his check-up while he sits on the couch with Eli watching tractor restoration videos, something they love to yet rarely get to do with William's demanding office job and pastoring the church.

"Hi ..." I balk at the reception desk. I don't have an appointment. I don't want to talk to anybody. I don't want to confirm that I'm pregnant. Why am I here?

"Do you have an appointment?" The plump blonde smiles and readies her long gold and black nails at the keyboard.

"Uh, no. But I think I'm pregnant."

"Oh. Do you need a test, or are you wanting to make an appointment? Do you know how far along you are? When was your last cycle?"

"Um ..." Nausea punches my stomach. Emotion clogs my brain.

"Are you alright?"

"No." The admission feels cathartic, and I blurt, "I already have three kids, and..." I adjust James on my hip. "...my baby is only eleven months old. I–I'm not sure what to do."

Her eyes turn sympathetic. "Go sit down for a minute. I'll get you some things."

I obey. As I repeatedly try to stop James from gnawing the magazine table, a terrifying memory creeps up. Unlike my easy pregnancy with Eli, James' brought an agonizing complication. He had hung out so low that he had cut off the blood flow to my right leg. A vein that ran the entire length of my leg had darkened and enlarged more and more for six of the nine months. If I stood still or sat for more than a minute, it would shoot fire or numbness through the whole leg. It had made trying to sleep or relax difficult and going to a normal church service impossible. It had hurt without reprieve, but it hadn't become dangerous until the last few weeks.

I shake my head. I can't think about those last few weeks right now. Those weeks planted in me a dread of carrying another baby.

What if this next one is even lower? What if both my legs are affected? What if the blood to my heart gets cut off? What if we both—no. Stop. Just stop.

I focus my attention on unlatching *Better Homes and Gardens* from James' grasp and mouth.

Oh, God, I can't go through that again.

Papers rustle, and I look up from James. The receptionist holds out a folder. "This has phone numbers of our offices and some other information." She hands it to me. "And a test and a packet of peppermint tea." She winks. Apparently, she can smell my peppermint oil.

"Thanks."

She gives me one last sympathetic smile then walks back to her desk.

I stare down at the folder with the hospital's name and a pregnant lady printed on it.

No. No, I can't risk that again.

I tuck James under my arm like a football so he can't reach my hair, and I head for the elevator.

•••

Once in the car, I let James crawl around the back while I rifle through the folder. It isn't worth it to strap him in until just before I start the car. He hates his car seat and screams every second he's in it.

I start scanning all the informational papers I already read while pregnant with Eli and James. A pamphlet falls into my lap. I stare at it.

Termination.

I never believed I would even entertain the thought of terminating a pregnancy, but as James finds my hair, yanks it, then gives me a wet willy and takes up a round of screaming for no reason, I do consider it.

They've made it legal in our state at all stages now.

William doesn't know yet.

It's still really early.

No one knows.

Everybody says it's just a mass of cells this early.

I don't even know if I am pregnant.

But I do know.

I can smell James's diaper way too keenly for the test to be wrong or to sit in the parking lot any longer. I call the clinic on the termination paper, schedule a phone consultation during nap time on Monday, and wrestle a screaming James into his safety harness.

I start the car but stare out the windshield.

Oh, God, I'm sorry. But I have to.

I cry all the way home.

•••

That afternoon Eli skips his nap because he's too excited about Dada being home, then Richard won't stop talking during dinner, all three kids end up dumping more food on the floor than they eat, Eli and Richard's bickering catapults James into a raging fit, no one can find Eli's favorite truck, and everyone but Dada cries through the bedtime story. After seeing Richard to his room after a fight over who gets to take *The Very Hungry Caterpillar* to bed, William tries to console Eli, and I go to our room and sit on the bed while nursing James.

That word on the pamphlet keeps flashing in my mind and threatening to make me sick.

God, I'm sorry, but I have to, I pray. *I mean, a third pregnancy won't be good for anyone. I almost didn't make it through with James, and when I was so sick, and then in the hospital, and then home with the broken rib, I couldn't do anything. I couldn't make food, or change a diaper, or pick up Eli. William even had to dress me. I couldn't take care of any of them, and I made life harder for everyone. I would be useless if anything like that happened again—or if I was even just normal first trimester sick.*

And I'm such a mean pregnant lady. I screamed at Richard and his siblings so much, and I got mad at William for the dumbest stuff. And my mom—I was even a troll to her when she just asked if I could update her scrapbook of Eli. Oh, God, and I can't get anything done with just these three. I'm behind on my work, I'm failing at potty training Eli, I don't have enough energy for Richard, and I don't even have time to take a shower most days. And all the expenses and appointments, God. I know William has a good pay between both jobs, and we're doing fine now, but he already has to take off so much work for all the boys' appointments and for pastoring the church.

That last thought cuts deep.

God, I'm a pastor's wife. I should know this isn't right, I do know this isn't right, but...God, I'm so tired of being exhausted and sick and being this mean person who yells at her kids and can't handle being a mom. And, God, I'm scared. I'm scared that I will die of I go through that again. I'm scared of being useless to William and the kids. I'm scared I'll become someone who none of them love or even know. I'm scared I'll fail at being a mom even worse than I am now if this pregnancy goes on. It has to be more responsible to end this and save my family from me not being able to do anything and being a hormonal banshee. It has to be.

I don't want to terminate the pregnancy, but I cannot handle any more kids. The chaos, screaming, fighting, and messes never stop. It's overwhelming. I'm not myself. It's sapping all my life and joy away. It may take my life.

I have to do it. I have to keep that appointment and terminate this pregnancy.

"Mama."

I sit up and blink around. James is gone, and Eli stands by the bed. William must have put James in his crib as he usually does when I fall asleep holding him, and Eli must have snuck out of their shared room during the transfer.

"Mama, come here." Eli reaches up to me.

Guessing he wants to go potty, I slide out of bed, take his hand, and let him lead me to our master bathroom.

"Mama, why you sad?"

I halt.

I'm standing by Eli, but I'm also sitting on the edge of the tub crying. William is kneeling in front of me. I notice that the silver that has started to tint the thick dark brown hair above his ears and in his beard isn't there. I start to think how he and Eli look so much alike when his hand picks up the object lying across my hands. He places a negative test in the trash can on the floor.

I remember this.

"Hey." He wraps me in a hug. "Even if we never have kids, I already have everything I want," he tells me, and he means it. "I married you knowing this."

The past me nods and sobs, "I–I just feel so...so broken. Like something's wrong with me. Something *is* wrong with me. I'm sorry I can't...can't give you kids."

He holds me close and assures me, "No, it's not something you, or I, or anybody controls. Whether or not we have kids is up to God. That's it."

"Mama." Eli tugs my hand. I stare at his face—the face of a miracle we waited ten years for and believed never would be possible. I had felt like such a horrible failure at being a woman because I couldn't have kids, and we never understood why God wouldn't let us. Then after all but two foster kids had gone, Eli came. He had made me more than I knew I ever could be. He had made me Mama. And while raising him, I realized those six kids had added so much to who I was and prepared me for my miraculous, strong-willed, deep loving, wild little Eli.

Eli tugs my hand. "Mama, God made me."

I gasp and jolt.

"It's okay," my husband whispers as he lifts James from my arms to take him to his crib.

I let my head fall back against the propped-up pillow.

"Crazy pregnancy dreams," I breathe, but it had been more memory than dream. I try to push out of my mind the memories of every negative pregnancy test. They rip at such deep wounds yet at the same time contrast so sharply with the fresh joy I had felt when I held Eli in my arms for the first time and knew the miracle wasn't just an empty hope. I yearn to forget all of it because those emotions stir up too much confusion.

Oh, Lord, I'm so thankful for Eli and how he is the proof that anything is possible with you. But, God...Oh, God, I'm horrible. We struggled so long with not being able to have a baby, and now I'm trying to get rid of one. What's wrong with me? But, God, it's different. It is. We have three now. Another one would be four, and that feels so close to the six foster kids, and that was too much. That was horrible. I hated waking up each day knowing what we'd face. I'm sorry, but I did.

My mind drifts through those difficult days.

The oldest boy threatens to slit William's throat. The two youngest girls scream and cry while clinging to one another as the caseworker tells them that they will not go home. The second youngest boy throws his V.B.S. dinner plate at the kitchen workers then roars curse words at them. Little Richard, because he doesn't want to take his nap, repeatedly hits and kicks me so hard that he leaves bruises for weeks.

I jolt again.

Richard has wandered into our room. The kid sleepwalks, and it scares me every time I catch him standing randomly around the house.

"Ugh, Richard," I slowly, loudly groan, telling myself that he isn't three anymore and isn't going to hurt me. "Go back to bed."

"Okay, but...but I...I made something. I made something at school and...I made something."

"Okay." I roll my eyes and wiggle out from under the covers. With a hand on his shoulder, I steer him through the dim house. We reach his bedroom door, and he mechanically finishes the trip to his bed. I turn and nearly scream as Richard runs past me toward the kitchen.

I'm in the kitchen.

He holds out a black frame. "I made this at school!"

"Oh..." I watch my face freeze with hesitancy. "Yeah? Who is that?"

Though I can't see the picture from where I stand, I know it depicts a human with a giant smile and brown hair around her head like a lion, and I know that the first time I saw it, I couldn't tell if it was his biological mother or me.

"It's you!" he proclaims. "It says, 'I love Mom!'"

He called me mom. He said he loved me.

Behind Richard, my grinning husband mouths, "Give him a hug."

I snap out of my shock and give him a hug. I enjoy the fuzzy feeling of being called Mom by him, and I tell him that I love him too.

I wake up.

My bladder demands a bathroom trip.

Totally disoriented in the dark, I feel my way into the master bathroom and focus on reality.

That was just another crazy pregnancy dream.

But it had really happened. Last Mother's Day, he had thought of me as his mom more than his biological mother.

Richard had experienced me not as a mother by blood but as a person who cared for him like a mother despite his initial hatred of me. His presence had forced me to take on the role of Mom and all the responsibility that came with it. He had necessitated my mindset and actions change, and then he had chosen me as his mom before the court handed me that title. He had called me his even before I had pushed past the fear of the foster care system taking him and had let myself see him as my son.

After finishing in the bathroom and sipping a drink of water, I burrow back under the covers.

I lie awake, my brain too full of memories, emotions, and fears to let sleep take over.

God... I don't know what to say. *God, I love them so much, but another one... What if another kid makes me start to love one of them less, or neglect them, or forget about them? Lord, you know how much I lose track of James. I found a leaf and two ladybugs in his diaper. Two! I mean... God, I...I can't. Four would be too hard. Life is already so hard that it's barely living.*

I try to clear my mind, but an obnoxious beeping rouses me. Rolling my head, I see the monitors on my left, and excruciating pain hits me. I can't breathe, but I cough uncontrollably. I want to lie down, but my freshly broken rib screams at every movement. I want to fully sit up, but the enlarged vein in my leg burns and reminds me of the potentially fatal blood clot. I want to feel like myself, but I'm thirty-four weeks pregnant, trapped at the hospital, delirious with an array of illnesses that led to the cough that led to the broken bone, unable to move and stop my blood from clotting, and utterly alone.

And I'm so scared he is going to die.

God, please just let James be okay. Please just let me know he's okay.

Right on cue, James jigs in my belly.

All night, the nurses monitor him and tell me that he's perfectly healthy and moving like he's the happiest baby in the world.

That fills me with joy.

Though I'm at my lowest, feeling like I'm doing nothing but struggling to exist, my unborn baby reminding me that he is alive and is distinctly his own human even while in me brings me joy. It reminds me that though God has connected us in a miraculous way, God still is the maker and life giver to each of us. God has made and is sustaining the life in me. Keeping him alive does not depend on me. Keeping me alive doesn't depend on me. That knowledge restores my life.

My baby gives me life when I would otherwise be dead.

A lovely little tune plays.

"Good morning," William groans and shuts off the alarm "How'd you sleep?"

"Um...I had some crazy dreams. You?"

"I can't breathe out of my left nostril. This man flu is probably going to kill me."

I roll my eyes.

He smirks then goes to grind his coffee. While I use the bathroom then drift back to the bed to prop the pillows, I consider telling William that I'm pregnant. The memories God poured into my mind have shifted my heart. I've remembered that my sons have each added to me and made me a richer, deeper person: Aunt Iris, Mama, and Mom in addition to Iris. I've remembered that the hard days, though very real and overwhelming, are more temporary than the beautiful days of playing outside in the sunshine, dancing with Eli, tickling James as he squeals with delight, and hearing Richard say that he loves his new family and wants to be our son forever.

Even though the clarity God has given me has calmed my mind in this moment, I know I'll need William's help to not revert to drowning in my fears and emotions among all the hormones that it takes to grow another human inside me.

God, help me tell William.

While I'm still fussing with the pillows, William comes in the room with James. "Oh, Mama's not ready, Jammers." William clicks like a squirrel to distract James from the fact that breakfast isn't ready.

Climbing in the bed, I babble, "William, I...I think I'm ..."

"I know." He glances at the peppermint oil on my nightstand. "I saw you gag at me and my coffee. I'm highly offended." His teasing tone and wide smile tell me he is delighted. "So, is it a girl? Can we name her Willamina?"

"No, we can't. And it's too early to know that."

"I know. But I'm still going to call her Willamina." He hands me James.

My dread of another baby ebbs at his silliness. I joke back, "Willamina is an ugly name."

"Uh! Don't talk about our daughter like that."

We grin at one another, and then he kisses my forehead. "You are amazing, Iris."

As William brushes his teeth, I nurse James. I stare at my baby's soft, rosy cheeks, chubby fingers, and face that everyone says looks like mine.

God made him in me.

God chose me to be His mama.

He was alive the whole time.

He brought me joy every day despite the difficulty of pregnancy.

All three of our boys were planned by God, and God chose me—specifically *me*—to be their mama, not because I was a fantastic mom, but because God knew we all needed one another to grow and know God better.

I pet James' little head.

If I wasn't fit to be a mom and if this wasn't the right time for another pregnancy, God wouldn't have let this happen. Each of my boys have taught me so much about life and God, and the next baby will too. Each baby does bring me life and joy. Each baby has made me more of the Iris that God intended me to be since before I was born.

I close my eyes.

God, thank you for reminding me of what we've went through to get our boys and how much they mean to us. Thank you for reminding me of the sorrow of being unable to have kids, how you gave us each child at the right time, the privilege of being called and loved as a mom, and the truth that they have always been alive and bringing us joy that can overcome the darkest of times. Thank you that they have brought us closer to you.

God, having another baby and being pregnant again is going to be hard, and I'm scared of how I'll act and what will happen. But you chose me for this. Help me to hold on to that truth; you chose me for this, you chose the timing for this, and so I am the right mama for them, this is the right time for a new baby, and you can help me be the best mama and the best version of Iris for them—all four of them.

H.A. Pruitt is the Christian fantasy author of the Anelthalien Series. She lives with her herd of guinea pigs, her sarcastic husband, and her three sons. She never wanted to be an author and would have been content to remain unknown, but God decided that she would be perfect to hear the story of Anelthalien and share it with the world. Now H.A. Pruitt's goal in all she does and writes is to listen to, obey, and glorify God.

You can learn more about the author and her works at **https://www.hapruitt.com/**

MY DAUGHTER SAMANTHA

By PARKER J. COLE

There was nothing Judge Monica Greenway could do but wait.

Wait for the doctors. Wait for the nurses. Wait for news.

Wait for God.

Alone in the hospital waiting room, Monica sniffed and grimaced, all while trying to keep the scream lodged in her throat from leaking out like escaped air from a busted tank.

That odd antiseptic scent that always reminded her of blood that had been washed away, but never fully erased from the surface permeated the room. In the hundreds of criminal cases she'd overseen in her last eleven years, no matter how often blood was washed off by some means, it remained a permanent marker that life once existed there.

... the voice of thy brother's blood crieth unto me from the ground...

Fluorescent lights hummed above her, casting a lifeless glow over the uncomfortable plastic chairs. She sat on one of them, a hard, slippery bench that dug into the backs of her thighs. It squeaked as she moved trying to stay stationary while its edges bit into her as she leaned forward, elbows on knees. Her fingers were laced so tightly together that her knuckles had gone white.

...Samantha, sweetheart...

Her feet wouldn't stay still. They tapped against the floor and then stopped once she noticed she was doing it, only to start again seconds later as her mind was again occupied by scenarios of what had been and what could be.

What *had* been?

Samantha standing on the auditorium stage, her graduation cap slightly askew, her smile wide and toothy as she delivered her valedictorian speech. Her large brown eyes so different from her own hazel ones had shone with nervous excitement.

What *had* been?

Samantha's smile disappearing as her face went slack and her eyes rolled in the back of her head. The stomach-flopping sight of

Samantha's body hitting the polished floor. Collective gasps from the crowd, the scrape of chairs as people rushed toward her, voices overlapping in panic.

And that single whisper.

"Mom?"

Then ... nothing.

Monica swallowed hard, forcing back the bile that crept up her throat.

A voice broke through the haze of her thoughts.

"Mrs. Greenway?"

Her head jerked up. The sound of her married name felt wrong. But she had no time to correct or care.

A young man stood before her, his white coat crisp, his badge clipped to the lapels of his coat.

...why are all the doctors so young?

She stood too quickly, her legs nearly buckling beneath her.

"Doctor, my daughter, Samantha?" Her voice cracked and she gripped her elbows and squeezed.

"Mrs. Greenway, your daughter suffered a severe episode of acute anemia. Her red blood cell count is low, which is why she collapsed. We've stabilized her for now, but she's in critical condition."

"What does that mean? What do you need to do?"

"She needs a blood transfusion. Without it, her organs will begin shutting down. We've started preparing, but there's a further complication."

Her pulse pounded in her ears, and she was having difficulty breathing. "Complication?"

He gave a curt nod, but his eyes were warm. "Samantha has a rare blood type—HH, also known as the Bombay phenotype."

"I'm aware of that," she interrupted with a shaky movement of her hand. "But what does that have to do with—"

"We don't have that blood type in our immediate supply."

A cold chill swept her body, and her legs lost their strength, crumbling and collapsing onto the chair once more.

"Oh, dear God."

The doctor came and sat beside her. She was aware of his presence but couldn't feel anything beside the needle-like dread piercing her flesh, her soul.

"We've already put out an urgent request to the blood bank, but there are few registered donors with this type."

Monica's stomach clenched. She should have known things were never simple.

"Do you know if Samantha's father has been tested for his blood type?"

Monica's breath stilled in her chest. Samantha's father.

"He has," she said slowly. "But he's not a match either."

Her eyes shut and she whispered the last words. "But her mother may be."

She could feel the doctor's shock even though she wasn't looking at him. Everyone always reacted the same way when the terrible secret that had been a part of her life for so long was forced to be given the light.

"Oh, I didn't know that—"

"Most people don't," she said curtly.

"Is there any way we can get in contact with her ... birth mother?"

Monica's felt the release of tension leave her shoulders. At least the young doctor had tact.

"It's possible. But how much time do we have before ..."

"Hours," he said, the word a blow that slammed into her stomach. "Samantha's hemoglobin levels are low. Without a transfusion, she may go into organ failure."

Hours.

... be sure your sin will find you out...

Her lips trembled, and she clenched her fists together. "I'll see what I can do."

•••

Monica sat in the dimly lit home office, the desktop cluttered with dozens of newspaper articles. Some were old and brittle with a yellowish tinge while others were newer but still showing signs of aging with the curled ends and wrinkled folds.

Her hands shook as she unfolded one newspaper clipping she had kept hidden for years.

The bold stark headline stared back at her.

MISSING: INFANT GIRL ABDUCTED FROM HOSPITAL

Beneath it was a grainy, black-and-white photograph of a swaddled newborn, her tiny face barely visible, her birth name printed below in stark, unfeeling ink.

Anaya Devi Patel.

Monica swallowed hard, her throat tight.

Seventeen years had passed, and yet the article still made her hands sweat. She had read these words a thousand times, but tonight—tonight, the words took on a cruel significance.

MISSING: INFANT GIRL ABDUCTED FROM HOSPITAL

The Washington Post – June 14, 2007

Boston, MA – Authorities remain baffled
in the case of Anaya Devi Patel, a
newborn girl from Massachusetts
General Hospital late last night.
Anaya, the daughter of Dr. Arvind and
Asha Patel, was born prematurely at
twenty-six weeks, weighing 4 lbs, 4 oz.
She was taken from the hospital's NICU
unit. The Patels, a prominent Boston

> *family, are well-known in the medical and business communities. Dr. Arvind Patel, a leading cardiothoracic surgeon at Massachusetts General, and Asha Patel, a corporate attorney and philanthropist, have pleaded for the return of their child, citing the dangers of abducting a baby still in need of medical care.*

Her fingers swept over the words, and a wet splash landed on the letters, seeping the paper.

...none of you understand...

The article went on with a desperate plea from the child's birth parents. A crime that had never been solved.

Her crime.

Monica exhaled shakily. Her life, career, and reputation had been built on a foundation of silence.

...she was always meant to be mine...

But now—now she needed the woman she had stolen from.

She forced herself to read the last line of the article, one she had always avoided.

If you have any information about the whereabouts of Anaya Devi Patel, please contact the Patel family at the number below.

Her gaze dropped to the faded phone number.

Wrong.

She reached for her phone with trembling fingers. The device felt as heavy as a brick for some reason, as if her fingers had lost all strength to hold anything. She flinched at the brightness of the screen.

This was it.

With a deep, shuddering breath, she entered the correct number and pressed *dial.*

The ringtone droned in her ear, each second stretching into eternity. Monica almost hung it up after the third ring, but then her grip on the phone tightened. She didn't have the option to let this opportunity slipped by. Didn't have the luxury of letting the past stay buried in obscurity.

Her daughter's life was in danger and her mother ...the woman who gave her birth ... was the only one who could save her.

A click.

"Hello, Attorney Patel speaking."

Monica's throat tightened. "It's me. Judge Greenway."

Silence.

"Judge Greenway," Asha Patel said at last. It was evident that she was the last person she ever expected to hear from.

That had been the deal anyway.

"What are you doing calling me?"

Monica closed her eyes. "I need to speak to you."

"I don't believe you do, judge," Asha replied with icy, almost cutting disdain. "We were never supposed to speak to each other again."

Monica forced down the lump in her throat. "This is an emergency."

Silence again.

"What about?"

...the secret we've kept for all this time...

Monica gripped the edge of the desk and squeezed.

"That's what I need to talk to you about," she said, trying to keep the sheer panic at bay. "Where can we meet?"

"I prefer nowhere. I prefer this call would end and I could go back to what I was doing."

Monica shook her head. "If wishes were curses..." she murmured. "We need to meet. Within the hour."

"The hour? Do you know how busy I am? If this is some kind of blackmail attempt after all this time—"

"No," Monica interrupted. "It's not that. But I can't say anything over the phone. You have to meet me. Now. There's very little time."

Another silence.

"Meet me at the statue in the square," Asha finally said in a cool, almost detached voice. "I'll be waiting."

Monica's grip on the phone slackened, and it slipped from her grasp, tumbling onto the table with a dull thud.

She had spent years hiding behind her success, her power, her reputation. But now, the past was coming to collect its due.

None of that mattered. Her daughter Samantha needed her.

...no matter what, you are her mother...

Why did that sound so hollow now? She couldn't save her daughter's life. All the love, care, and devotion. All the sacrifices, and the triumphs. All of it meant nothing when they didn't share the same blood.

Only Samantha's real mother did.

•••

The city square bustled with activity, but under the bronze statue of some important figure, Monica waited. Sunshine flooded the area along with the cacophony of smiling faces, laughter, and children playing nearby.

Monica stood in his shadow, her arms crossed tightly over her chest as if she could hold herself together when everything about her wanted to flail out.

How could things be so cheerful when her daughter lay in the balance between life and death?

The wind toyed with her hair, whipping strands into her eyes, she pushed them back, before someone came into her field of vision.

Asha Patel.

She hadn't changed. Not really. Brown skinned with ageless features that could make her anywhere from early twenties to her forties. Power radiated from the top of her loose, bun-styled hair to the bottom of her Louboutin high heels.

When she came abreast of her, but standing a few feet away, Asha said in a sharp tone, "You have sixty seconds before I walk away, Judge Greenway."

"It's about Anaya," she said quickly. "She needs a blood transfusion. And she needs it now."

Asha's eyes flickered. "Anaya is dead."

Monica let out a deep breath. "No, she isn't." She swallowed, forcing her voice to steady. "She's alive, seventeen years old, and valedictorian of her high school class."

Asha's cool, hard face melted slowly to one of shock. "You're not serious!"

Monica shook her head. "I am. Her name is Samantha Greenway."

The slap came so fast, Monica never saw it coming.

"You—"

The insult was drowned out by the blood pounding in Monica's ears. A sting exploded across her cheek and her head snapped to the side.

Hot, tingling pain.

A few people nearby turned their heads at the sound of the impact, but Monica barely registered them.

She didn't move to defend herself.

Didn't lift a hand to her cheek.

She deserved this. Every bit of it.

"I'm sorry."

Asha turned away, her steps faltered as she made her way toward a black wrought-iron bench near the edge of the square and all but collapsed onto it.

Monica slowly followed her, knowing that the ashen look on the other woman's face was her fault. Monica sat beside her, careful to leave enough space between them.

Asha shook as if she sat in the grip of a winter wind.

"I'm sorry, Asha."

•••

An invisible ice wind had come and taken Asha captive, ravaging her body so that she couldn't stop shaking. From the tips of her toes to the crown of her head, every part of her trembled as if the nerves themselves were caught in some wild, frenetic dance.

This can't be real.

She stole a glance at Monica Greenway, and something hot and spiked ripped through her body.

You. Lied. To. Me.

Red filled her vision, while bile bubbled at the back of her throat. She was going to be sick.

"Asha, please."

She held up a hand. The last thing she wanted Monica Greenway to do was speak to her.

Inside, something wailed and clawed at her brain.

My daughter, Anaya!

The worst moment in her life played up before her, unfurling like the edges of a scroll. She saw herself once again in their house, she and Arvind glaring at each other in the doorway of the vestibule that led to the outer entrance.

"Asha, please. We'll be fine."

Arvind's brown eyes searched hers, pleading for her to reconsider. For a moment, Asha hesitated, seeing the desperation in his eyes fight against her resolve. But then she shook her head.

"No, we won't be. We're not ready for this."

"We'll never be ready, Asha." His voice sharpened as his hand cut through tension in the air. "Even if we had all the money in the world, we'd still find reasons to wait. Think about it. No one is ever ready. We'll adapt."

"Adapt?" A bitter laugh escaped her. "Arvind, we've been over this. I just started at the prosecutor's office three months ago. It's not the right time."

"I make enough to take care of us," he insisted. "Just take a few years off, and then you can go back to work."

"We can't afford a child."

"Yes, we can. We'll figure it out."

"No, we won't." Her pulse pounded. "And if you can't see that—"

"It's not me who's refusing to see." Arvind pressed his thumb and forefinger into his eyes and squeezed them shut. After a moment, he removed his hand and lifted his gaze to her.

She knew what he was going to say before he did. That was something he'd always liked about her, one of those quirks that drew him in.

"That's my baby, too."

Even though she knew he was going to say that, at the utterance of those words, Asha stilled. Something hot singed her skin. "Your baby?"

"We made this child together." His gaze softened, almost reverent. "When you told me, I was happy. You know I've always wanted to be a father."

"Yes, but not now." Her hands clenched. "Besides, you're not the one who has to carry this child for months. You're not the one whose body will never be the same, whose career will be derailed, whose entire life will be—"

"I know," he interrupted, his voice raw. "I know it's unfair. But you are the lifebringer, Asha. That's the reality." His fingers dragged through his silky black hair. "No one ever said it was fair."

The words sliced through her.

When Asha had discovered she was pregnant, it was a shock. Her life was finally lining up with her aspirations. A baby would interfere with everything. It's not that she didn't ever want children. She just didn't want them right now.

She knew eventually she would have to tell Arvind about the baby. It was surprisingly easy to keep it from him because they were both busy with their separate careers. But that also made it easier to procrastinate. And all that time, her baby continued to grow inside her.

When she finally told Arvind months later, he'd been ecstatic and looking forward to having a family. "May God bless your womb," he'd softly to her as they lay in bed, his head resting on her slightly swelled stomach. "May God help us to raise our child to fear Him."

It was a tender moment, and yet, trepidation coursed through her like tiny shards of glass. She still didn't want this baby. But how could she forbid Arvind his right to be a father?

How could she put aside her life for a child she didn't want?

Every time she told Arvind that she didn't want the baby, he'd convinced her to keep it. And for a while she lied to herself. About her feelings. About her wishes. About loving the child growing within her when all she could think was that she didn't want it. Not now.

Then, one day, she saw a clinic gleaming in the sunlight like a beacon of hope. Without thinking, she pulled into the parking lot and went inside, barely realizing what she was doing, but driving by a need, a desire to ... to...

That was when she met Monica Greenway. A nurse who had stood next to the doctor while she asked question after question. And they told her what she wanted to hear.

"... we're one of the few who can perform the procedure ..."

"... you don't have to explain. You have to do what's best for you..."

Monica had escorted her out the door and squeeze her shoulder reassuringly. "Mrs. Patel, you come back when you're ready. We'll be here to help you."

Help you.

Those two words haunted her as she drove back home, saying nothing to Arvind as he bought nursery furniture and had a crew come into the house and start building and designing the nursery room.

Teddy bears and trains decorated the walls. Soft greens and yellows. A crib that would fold into a bed eventually. Toys stuffed in boxes.

Arvind beaming and excited. Eyes filled with joy.

Every night before they went to bed, he prayed over her womb, and kissed the skin, raining blessings on her. Gathering her in his arms and telling her how much he loved her.

"Thank you for this," he'd said.

Still, the indecision remained.

Then weeks later, when she was almost seven months along, she woke up and knew. She just knew...

"I can't do this," she whispered in the morning stillness with Arvind's light snoring beside her in bed. "I can't. I can't. I can't."

The words followed her as she went to court, and met with witnesses and officers.

I can't. I can't.

Then she remembered Monica' s words. "Help you."

She called the clinic that day and Monica answered the phone.

"I need you to help me," she said desperately, her hands gripping the phone hard, making her knuckles pale.

"Of course," Monica answered. "But you have to hurry. And we'll have to claim a health exception to have this done when you're this far along."

"Fine," Asha insisted, anxiety fueling her insistence. "Let's claim a health exception. We have to do this right away!"

By the time she reached the clinic two hours later, her hands were trembling. Arvind's words echoed in her mind, refusing to be silenced.

"I know it's unfair. But you are the lifebringer, Asha. That's the reality."

The words followed her as she walked down the hallway, the lights above casting an eerie ghostly glow above her.

Is it fair to the baby within her?

Is it right to make this decision without Arvind?

Of course it is! I'm not ready. We can always have another baby later.

But what about this one?

The questions swirled in her mind as the medical professionals helped her onto the table, took her clothes and prepared her for the procedure. All the while, she kept remembering Arvind's joy at becoming a father. It broke her heart, but she couldn't stop now. She was almost free!

During the procedure, she heard a sound. It was faint, tremulous even, but she heard it.

A baby's cry.

Her heart thudded in her chest, slamming away as it increased the beeps from the medical machinery monitoring her.

Her baby cried.

Oh God! Oh God! Oh God!

"Stop! Please stop!"

The doctors and the nurses said things, but she could barely hear them from the recurring sound of the baby's cry.

Her baby cried.

"Please stop! Don't do this."

Her anxiety overwhelmed her and she blacked out. When she opened her eyes moments later, the baby's cry was gone. And she saw the sad, hazel eyes of the woman she would eventually know as Monica Greenway gazing at her from above the surgical mask as she shook her head.

And Asha cried and cried and cried.

She shuddered out of the memory and through her blurry vision saw the pathetic expression on Monica's face. "How could you do this to me?"

•••

"You told me she was dead." Asha choked on the words, coughing.

Monica glanced away. "I know. Look, we were in gray areas back then. The regulations and oversight weren't nearly what they are now. She was born alive, but she stopped breathing and I thought that was over. Then, all of sudden, she started to breathe and cry. It was a miracle. Then I knew she was meant to be mine. *My* daughter."

"You *lied* to me!" Asha hissed.

"I know!" Some part of her flared inside. "But let's not pretend you wanted the baby. You were willing to terminate her to pursue your career."

"I was twenty-three years old, newly married, and just out of law school. I thought having a baby would —"

"'— be a nuisance and a hindrance,'" Monica interrupted, quoting what Asha had said all those years ago. "You lied to the clinic and the state. You claimed your life was in endangered by continuing the pregnancy...which is illegal. All to be run away from your responsibilities to your daughter." She frowned at the thought. Bitterly, she added, "I just gave you what you wanted."

Asha flinched as if Monica had struck her.

A grim smile came to Monica's lips. "You had *everything*, Asha Patel. A rich husband who loved you, a promising career. And a baby."

She had been around hundreds of terminations over the years, at various stages. Young women, older women, poor women and those in between. This had been the first time in her experience that she'd seen a woman who had everything want to throw her child away. And so far into the pregnancy.

"But when the baby survived the abortion, I changed my mind," Asha asserted.

Asha's words brought Monica out of the reverie. "Did you?"

“I did! I thought that God had given me another chance to do the right thing. But then you said—”

“I said the baby died of complications from the abortion,” Monica finished for her.

She would always remember that day, years ago, when she looked at the small, pitiful baby. The one who should have died but hadn’t. A little girl struggling to breathe, to live. Her own mother had already abandoned her, even before the lie. Monica already loved this struggling child. She would bring her to full health and be the mother this girl deserved.

When she glanced back at Asha, she saw hatred in the woman’s brown eyes ... so much like Samantha’s.

Pure, undiluted, searing hatred.

Asha’s voice trembled with barely restrained fury. “Why? How could you *do* that to me?”

“Because I couldn’t have any children!” Monica screamed. “You may have carried her, but you were no mother!”

Asha’s red-rimmed eyes widened. “You *lied* to me.”

“She was in the NICU for weeks. Weeks! Clinging to life and all I could do was pray for her to live. There were times when I thought she wasn’t going to make it. I prayed to God that she would because I would raise her as my daughter and she would be mine. My husband had left me for another woman. But he refused to grant me a divorce because it was more convenient for his Don Juan lifestyle.” She sighed before continuing. “Asha, I wanted her so badly! All the money you gave me went toward her.”

Even to her own ears, it sounded so trite. So insensitive. She had seen the profound look of relief on Asha’s face when she heard the baby’s cries. She’d seen that hidden joy and knew that Asha wanted her child. But she had stolen that chance from the other woman. Lied. Manipulated. Exploited her moment of weakness.

Did she feel sorry for that? Even after all this time, Monica wasn't sure.

•••

Back then, to protect her and Arvind's reputation, Asha had pulled strings and money had greased palms. The newspaper article had reported the child abducted from a hospital instead of an abortion clinic. If the truth had come out, she wouldn't have just lost her career — she would have gone to prison.

It had been hardest to explain to Arvind. If there was ever a time she saw anger in her husband's eyes, it was then. They were dark like black ice, and she was sure he hated her.

His hushed, pained voice made his accusations so much worse. "You panicked and went to get an abortion," he glowered. "At twenty-six weeks into the pregnancy. Without telling me!" Arvind had never raised his voice at her before. It shamed her.

She wanted to soothe his heartache, but she had nothing to offer. Everything he'd said was true. "She was alive!" she exclaimed. "The abortion didn't work...at first." Her spirits fell further. "But she was too young, too weak. She didn't make it."

Arvind grabbed the newspaper from the kitchen table and shook it in his hand at her. "And do you want to explain this, *too?"*

The headline taunted her: ***MISSING: INFANT GIRL ABDUCTED FROM HOSPITAL***

"I...I did that to protect us," she weakly deflected.

"To protect yourself, you mean!"

"No! I was protecting you, too!" she insisted. "If the truth got out, if could have damaged your career."

He simmered before replying, "There would have been no risk if you'd just carried the baby to term." She marveled at how such a calm voice could hold so much anger. "You risked far more than you know."

She sat down on the plush sofa, her strength fading like her resolve. "Are you leaving me then?" she said with a defeated tone.

"No," he answered, his anger slipping into disappointment. "I still love you, Asha. But I will need some time to come to terms with this."

She couldn't argue with that. As he exited the room to go to the study, she began to cry, grieving over her scarred marriage and her lost daughter.

•••

Monica had told herself she was *helping*. That she had saved everyone from scandal, from disgrace. That she had given the child—*her* child—a real chance at life. She'd left the clinic, both to protect it and because she could no longer perform the service when she had received her own mixed blessing.

Her husband refused to come home but allowed her to spend money from their account as she saw fit. She used it to stay home with Samantha in her early years. Eventually, she was accepted into law school and became a lawyer before becoming a judge.

All the while, her secret remained safe.

Until now.

"She was *my* daughter," Asha said coldly.

Monica opened her mouth to naysay that but then closed it. Wasn't Asha right? Samantha *was* her biological daughter. And now, she was the only one who could save Samantha's life.

Asha's voice was barely above a whisper. "Tell me everything."

Monica told her, leaving nothing out.

"I see," Asha said when she finished the tale. "So, the only one who can save her is me."

"If you wish to," Monica said.

Asha leapt to her feet. "If I wish to? Are you out of your mind? The gall!"

Monica flinched at the venom in her tone, but she didn't look away.

Because this was justice.

This was the punishment she had evaded for seventeen years. In her life as a judge, she had meted out punishment according to the law, knowing full well that she had broken a moral law.

Stolen a child from its rightful mother.

"Does she know?" Asha asked.

Monica hesitated and then sighed. "No."

Asha let out a sharp, humorless laugh. "Of *course*, she doesn't."

A beat of silence.

Then, when Asha finally turned back, her expression had changed.

The fury was still there, but underneath it was something else.

A mother's instinct.

A mother who had just learned her child was alive.

A mother who—no matter how much she despised the woman before her—was already making a decision.

"Take me to my daughter, Monica," Asha said.

She would save Samantha.

Because that's what mothers did for their daughters.

•••

Her daughter was beautiful.

Perfect with the same facial structure as her father, and the same long hair as her mother. Her long lashes rested on her cheek bones, and she slept, snoring a little bit.

Her hand clutched her heart.

My daughter, Anaya.

Monica was the only one she told what her daughter's name would be and she promised to always remember.

Rage once more poured into Asha's veins. Monica had stolen her daughter from her!

Had she?

The voice seemed to come from outside of herself. As if there was something speaking into her ear.

Had Monica stolen her daughter, or had her daughter been restored to her?

Asha's mouth fell open at the thought. After what she thought was Anaya's death, she learned that she and Arvind could not have any more children. The procedure had done something to her that made her sterile.

The added pain of that news, combined with her own deceptive actions, had pushed their marriage to the brink, almost past saving. But they eventually moved past it and rekindled their love. But the old pain had always laid between them like a multi-colored elephant in the room. Sometimes, almost twenty years later, she'd come upon Arvind holding the image of Anaya's ultrasound, smiling sadly.

He'd always wanted to be a father.

He is a father, the voice outside of herself said. *He is Anaya's father.*

And I'm her mother.

Tears welled in Asha's eyes, blurring her vision, the miracle of her daughter. She was alive. And she needed help only Asha could give.

When the blood transfusion had started, Asha would have given every drop for her daughter. It was the thing she could do.

...you are the lifebringer, Asha. No one ever said it was fair.

Arvind's words echoed in her brain. She clasped a hand over her mouth. No, it wasn't fair. It was an honor, a duty, a blessing, a responsibility, a gift, a chore, a trial, an inconvenience, a pleasure, a pain.

It was everything. It was what a mother was.

Simple... everything.

Looking over at Monica, she could see a mother's love on that woman's face. She could see the same worry, the same care, the same ... love.

They had conspired together. And Monica had betrayed her. Their actions were illegal, unethical, horrible.

Still, her daughter was alive! Alive and now she would thrive again.

Because of her.

Was it God? Had God given her the opportunity to give her daughter life once more?

"Monica."

The woman glanced up at her, eyes glistening. "Yes?"

"Thank you for ... this."

"I'm so sorry, Asha."

"So am I," Asha said wearily. "May I take a picture of her? To show Arvind."

A frightened look came into Monica's face. Asha instantly knew why.

"There won't be any repercussions. No one knows and no one's *going* to know. Do you understand?"

Monica stared at her for a long time, and then she nodded.

Asha took out her phone and with tears streaming down her face, took a picture of her daughter, Anaya.

No, not Anaya.

Samantha.

At that moment, the girl started to stir and Asha's heart leaped into her throat.

She was waking up!

Should she run? Leave? Stay?

Samantha's eyes fluttered opened and she croaked out, "Mom?"

•••

The steady *beep* of the heart monitor was the first thing Samantha heard as she came out of the dark cloud she'd been under.

She felt warm like she was wrapped in a heavy blanket.

Her eyelids fluttered open, and for a moment, everything was too bright. She flinched.

"Mom?"

A shadow moved into her periphery. "Sweetheart, I'm here."

Samantha turned her head slowly, vision adjusting as she saw her mother sitting at her bedside, her normally poised and confident face was worn and stamped with dark circles under her eyes.

"Thirsty," she croaked out.

Monica came forward with a cup in her hand. "Here, sweetheart."

Samantha swallowed, the cool relief easing the dryness in her throat. She tried to speak, but her voice came out as a hoarse whisper. "What... happened?"

"You collapsed at your graduation." Monica brushed a stray lock of hair from Samantha's forehead. "You were anemic. Your body wasn't producing enough red blood cells, and you needed a transfusion."

Samantha's brow furrowed. "A transfusion?"

Monica hesitated. A second too long.

Another movement caught Samantha's attention, and she turned to see a woman standing in the doorway of the hospital room. She had deep brown skin, and dark, intense eyes. Her hair was pulled into a neat bun, and though her face was calm, her posture was rigid.

Samantha frowned. "Who...?"

The woman stepped forward. "My name is Asha Patel."

Samantha looked between them—her mother, tired but watchful, and this stranger, whose gaze held something she couldn't quite name.

Something was wrong.

Monica cleared her throat and shifted in her chair. "Samantha, the blood transfusion you needed—your blood type is extremely rare." She exhaled, glancing at Asha before continuing. "There was only one person, er, locally who could donate their blood in time to save you."

Asha's dark eyes never left Samantha's face.

It was her.

"You?" Samantha asked, voice raspy.

Asha nodded once.

A question formed in Samantha's mind, one that she didn't understand why she needed to ask.

Before she could, Monica inhaled sharply. "There's a reason why—"

Asha lifted her hand, stopping her.

Samantha noticed her mother stiffened like a board.

"I was a match," Asha said with what looked like a strained smile. "That's all that matters."

Tension filled the room, but Samantha didn't know why. "But... how?"

Asha gave a small, practiced smile. "Fate, perhaps?"

"Mom says Fate is simply the tool of God."

Asha and her mother shared another look, but her head started throbbing again and she groaned. "Mom, my head hurts."

"I'll get the nurse for you."

"No," Asha Patel interrupted. "I'll get her for you. You stay here with... your daughter."

Samantha noticed that her mother's mouth dropped in shock. Asha gave a small shake of her head, as if there was some kind of message going on between them.

"Thank you," Monica said after a moment. Samantha saw tears blur her mother's eyes.

"I hope you'll allow me to repay your kindness by ... coming by and visiting us when you can."

Now Asha looked shocked, and then she teared up. “I’d like that. Very much.”

Samantha laid back down and closed her eyes.

•••

Arvind gazed down at the picture Asha had given him, reeling from the extraordinary story his wife had shared.

His daughter was alive. She should have been dead, and yet, here she was alive and seventeen years old. It didn't matter that he didn't have a chance to be her father or experience all the things a father should.

She was alive and that was good enough for him.

"Do you still hate me?" Asha asked.

He peeled his eyes away from the picture, and looked into the depths of his wife's gaze, seeing the anguish, fear, sorrow. So much regret.

And a hint of joy.

"No. I never hated you, Asha."

It wasn't quite true. There had been some years where the hate had warred with the love within him. Not hatred of her, but at what she had done. How she'd taken the choice from him and made it all about her wants and needs.

Over time, he gave his hate and bitterness over to God. And all that was left was a new sort of love. It had been tested and tried, coming out refined like silver.

"But—"

Arvind took her in his arms and kissed her gently on the cheek, tasting the salt of her tears.

They would probably spend the rest of their lives, trying to eke out any kind of relationship they could have with their daughter.

It was enough to know she was here on this earth and that he was a father.

When they pulled apart, he glanced down at the image again.

"What's her name again?"

Asha told him and he repeated the words, seeing the years of loss being made up.

Quietly he said, “My daughter, Samantha.”

Parker J. Cole is a USA Today Bestselling author of historical romance, as well as a speaker, podcast host, and CEO of the podcast network PJC Media. As an author, Parker enjoys exploring history through the vehicle of romance. Her speaking topics focus on inspiration for aspiring authors. For over a decade, she has interviewed authors from all over the world via her podcast network. Consumed with a plethora of interests that keep her life busy, she lives in Detroit, Michigan. Visit her site at **https://www.parkerjcole.com**

PROMISED TO TOMORROW
By LAUREN SMYTH

I fell asleep next to a cold thermos of coffee, arms crossed under my head, a stray sheet of notebook paper whiffling in my breath.

I always wondered what would have happened if I'd stayed awake. If I'd drunk the coffee earlier. If I'd spent six hours in bed instead of four. If I had all my wits about me when Christophe came back from dinner.

The six-person library table was angled awkwardly against the window, crisscrossed with laptop cables and streaks of dying sunlight. Towers of medical textbooks, edges ragged with notes, cast shadows on the floor. One of my friends had mashed a row of chewing gum against the window—her characteristically vulgar method of tracking how long we'd been studying. I'd have to clean it up later, since I was the freshie. But that was a small price to pay for being one with the coveted group.

I had a notebook under my head. A student's favorite pillow. It had a dark green cover bound with gilt rings, and from the price on the back, you could tell it belonged to Christophe. Each page was color-coded in marker along the edge ("Anatomy I," "Calc III"). The date was written at the top right corner in frigid penmanship. No unreadable prescriptions from Chris. He was meticulous, and everyone said that was what would make him a good doctor. He got those scholarships not because he was really brilliant—not in the reckless genius sense, at least—but because he had never made a mistake.

Something stirred at my side. Blinking fog from my eyes, I raised my head, and a strand of unwashed hair crunched in my mouth.

"Sorry," I muttered, running a hand through my bangs. "I didn't think you'd be back so soon."

Just my luck.

I made a habit of not caring. Made things easier. Kept me from going insane. But I felt myself shrink under Christophe's coolly analytical gaze.

People who didn't know him were careful to avoid getting into the line of those eyes, unsettled—so they liked to say behind his back—by the way he seemed to see straight through skin to bone. That was a doctor's way, a real doctor's skill. What those people didn't realize was that Chris could also smile. And when he did, his eyes narrowed and crinkled, his cheeks reddened, and his face radiated a rare kind of gentleness. I'd heard it called *bedside manner.* I was pretty sure it was just the relics of Chris before he became jaded by ninety-hour weeks.

He placed a Styrofoam to-go box on the table in front of me. A heavenly smell wafted from the lid. Eggs, bacon, and buttery biscuit. Breakfast for dinner. *Carbs.* Good for the brain.

"It's better to fall asleep while studying than to do it in the middle of the exam," he said. "Trust me."

"Surely you never did that."

"Just once. Pharmacology."

I snorted. I could never relax that much.

He dropped cross-legged into the chair across from me, looping one arm over the back of our friend's seat. "I wanted to get back as quick as I could. Figured you'd prefer to eat your sandwich hot."

"Figured right." My family always warned me not to eat like a slob, but I guessed they had never really been hungry before. Nursing sapped the energy from your bones like a marathon.

"Lucie."

"Hm?" I said through a mouthful of egg and cheese.

"Hm," Chris echoed playfully. "Never mind. I don't want to interrupt your dinner."

Another bite. "What's wrong?"

"Nothing."

I put down the sandwich, still chewing, and reached for a tissue to wipe my fingers. A feeling of uncleanness had settled into my skin, as if I had arrived late to a test or forgotten my lines in an audition.

Tissue box there. My hand here. Sunset sweeping across brown eyes, illuminating the buttery softness of freckled skin. Chris's hand here, too, pressing mine onto the table. He leaned forward, sweeping the sandwich out of the way, and pressed his lips against mine.

That wasn't how I imagined my first kiss. Unprepared. Still chewing. Surrounded by the dueling scents of mold with hot printer paper and egg sandwich with Chris's cologne—something warm and deep and faintly spiced, like cider. His lips tasted bitter, and they were dry enough for me to feel their rough, wintry texture.

But that unlikely kiss was with Christophe. And Christophe was a forceful man, a take-charge-when-it-mattered kind of man. *Christophe* had wanted to kiss *me.* After it was over, I wished I could wipe my lips with the back of my hand.

That was real life. Not as romantic as the movies made it seem. I was no starry-eyed girl. I knew that much.

The next kiss was my idea. I reached across the table and pulled him in again, worming my hand free from his and draping it across his shoulder, pulling him closer, pressing our knees together under the table. I felt his lips move against mine:

"I've been wanting to do that."

I took my time nodding. Was this the college romance I'd dreamed of, hunting me down in the middle of the busiest season of my life? Was this what they meant when they said love would spark unexpectedly?

He pulled back. "I guess we're boyfriend and girlfriend now?"

It was all so sudden. So perfect, so delightful, but so unexpected. What had I done to make Christophe notice me? Couldn't it have been anyone? Why me?

Why me?

•••

"Actually." I paused.

Did I have to tell him? Was it ridiculous to make a big deal out of this when we'd been dating for less than a week? Chris had never minded that my best friend was the boy I'd known since freshman year of high school—had never said anything about it, anyway, though I'd mentioned it off-hand a few times. I thought he should know.

Though I hadn't missed the look on his face when I gave him my phone for directions and the text app happened to be open. Steven's name was at the top. Actually, in my phone, he went by "Four Hundred Duckpower Steve." Chris's eyes had darkened for a moment before he returned my phone and pulled out his own.

"Actually?" Steven prompted. A keyboard clicks in the background of his microphone. He's gaming again.

Something about the way he said it filled me with dread. I had to tell him. Explain that I was leaving something safe for something new. And why. A decision I realized, with a vague sense of discomfort, I could never entirely justify. This wasn't supposed to be a trade.

"I met someone." It came out in a rush. "I ... we're dating now. I don't know why I'm telling you this. It's just ... I thought you'd want to know."

Laughter filled the phone with static. Loud, boisterous, untroubled laughter. "Did you tell him about my shotgun collection?" Steven had always been delighted to play the older brother. I knew he would be, which for some reason made everything worse. "Tell him he's dead if he lets anything happen to you. Hey, for research purposes, what's his address? Where might I find this—"

"Your messages popped up the other day while we were on a date." Steven had sent me a photo of his latest hobby project, a full suit of armor crafted from pull tabs he'd scavenged from beach trash cans. "I'm afraid I can't talk to you as much, Steven. You understand. There's not so much time in nursing school, and … I don't know if Chris is comfortable with it. Chris is the guy that—he's my boyfriend. We're … ah."

I couldn't say why my sentence ended in a gulp. Perhaps it was because the silence between us had grown heavy, with surprise on Steven's end and dull finality on mine. My subconscious warned me that I had said something wrong. Wrong—or merely uncomfortable. No one wanted to have these kinds of conversations. But everyone must have had them. There wasn't such a thing as friends. There could never be such a thing between a boy and a girl.

"Understandable," Steven said at last. The keyboard had gone silent. "Reach out to me whenever you want. I'll try not to blow up your phone. But I'm always here if you need anything. Hey, while you're still on the line, how about those chain link gauntlets? I think I have enough materials left for both arms …"

I allowed myself those last moments. My finger left a greasy print on the red hang-up button, and I dropped my phone on my nightstand with the painful sensation that I had just cut off a family member for a man I barely knew.

But there couldn't be two. Not even if one of them was like a brother to me.

•••

There was B.C. and A.C.—Before Chris and After Chris. Before Chris there were joyous calls home to celebrate top grades. A.C., I realized I wouldn't be valedictorian.

Not that it mattered. My parents had always told me it didn't matter, that you couldn't compare coursework across majors. But my grades could have been better—*were* better B.C. If I was going to spend the rest of my life with this man, I could afford to make a few sacrifices.

It was roses on the weekends, which I dried and collected in a vase beside my bed. It was notes passed between campus mailboxes, written on gilt-edged stationery with penmanship like a computer font. It was stolen kisses and moments alone that turned into hours. It was patience with conflicting schedules, staying up to say goodnight, teary-eyed phone calls while Chris talked me down from post-exam jitters, hands held while Chris fought the stress of grueling, sleepless hours in residency.

Love was something big. It was making plans for the future before we had known each other two months, ignoring the cautious whisper at the back of my mind that the future was no man's. It was reassurance, promises that nothing would change, that life would always look like this. That we would still hold hands under the table while our friends talked and that we would stay together when our friends didn't and that we were different. We were meant to be, tied by the irrevocable red string of fate.

Love was so small that a single day of silence might have broken it entirely. I always wondered if Chris knew how much a good morning text meant to me. It meant that I was the first thing he thought of before he checked his schedule. Something about being his *first* and *only* felt right, but that kind of love required constant proof of its existence. Sometimes it was exhausting. More often it was elating, a stab of perfection in an otherwise dreary and gray and monotone world of sleep and study, study and sleep.

It was perfect. It was delicate. It was two years of my life.

Maybe that was why I was so reluctant to give it up.

•••

He hadn't gotten the cough drops. I tried to be gentle when I reminded him. Everyone was stressed. That was why I'd gotten sick. Chris was stressed, too. A patient had died last week, and it wasn't his fault. But I would never understand the strain. I hadn't asked him to bring me medicine, but he had offered, and I felt too sick to drive. My first mistake was accepting an offer made with reluctance, out of pity or obligation or something else I couldn't understand and had never felt around him.

Why was I in tears? Why was he screaming? Why were words spoken that he had promised never to use, and how could a head hurt so much, and when was I going to learn how to breathe again?

He brought the medicine the next day. A dozen roses and a handwritten apology note.

This will never happen again.

I promise.

•••

The study table was quiet. It was Chris's quietness, hanging over all of us like a snare. He sat across from me, shoulders hunched around his notebook, poring over a hand-drawn diagram of the endocrine system. Maybe I was imagining his anger. Maybe, when we had apologized to each other the day before, I was the one who hadn't entirely meant it. Maybe it was my fault things weren't right between us.

I was the woman. I was the gentler one. Empathy came naturally to me, I'd always been told, in a way that it didn't to men. If someone was going to apologize, it had to be me.

I waited until our friends left for lunch. Chris got up to follow them, ignoring me when I said I'd rather stay behind and eat what I packed.

"Please." I grabbed his wrist, averting my eyes in embarrassment. How could I be so fragile, so vulnerable? "We need to talk."

He stared at me, the familiar analytical wrinkles forming between his eyebrows.

"I'll be along shortly," he told the others.

They shrugged and continued toward the door. None of them looked back, and so none of them saw the single tear that slid free before I could blink it away.

"What?" Chris asked curtly, sliding into the seat across from me.

Chris had always responded to softness. He had always comforted me when I cried and held me until I could breathe again—until yesterday. What had been so different about yesterday?

Everyone fights, I reminded myself. *Does everyone fight like this?*

"I'm sorry," I blurted out, my eyes fixed on his notebooks. Why couldn't I look at him? "I shouldn't have given you anything else to do. I didn't mean to cause you stress. I ..."

I'd gotten good at leaving the ends of my sentences to the imagination. Some things, I was learning, were just too difficult to say.

I love you when you were angry. *I'm sorry* when you were wrong—or when you weren't. That was what happened when the hormones wore off. All relationships were bound to dry up eventually. And you learned to live in the desert.

"You've got to know the difference between a real offer and an attempt to be polite," Chris told me, leaning back in his chair and crossing his arms. "People don't always say what they mean. You knew I was busy. I stayed on the phone with you while I worked and had Steph bring you tea. How could you ask for anything else?"

How could you?

How could you?

I clasped my hands in my lap. I thought I'd asked for ten minutes—a pickup, a drop off, a few dollars to the campus pharmacy. The way Chris put it made me feel like I'd asked for a lifetime.

I would have given you mine, a timid voice at the back of my mind suggested. *I've done it in the past. I'd do it again.*

But I was a nurse. Not a very good nurse, by my grades. I had all the time in the world compared to the medical residents, and no one's life depended on the deftness and the gifting and the training contained in my hands. I couldn't compare Chris's efforts to mine.

"Chris," I ventured, "do you still love me?"

He let out a sigh. I felt myself shrink deeper into my chair.

"Of course I do," he said gently. "I'm sorry you feel neglected. Let's forget about this and try again tomorrow, okay, my pretty nurse?"

He held out his hands and I gave him mine, waiting for the little pattern of squeezes we used to communicate affection when our gossip-seeking friends were around. But it didn't come. Instead, he stroked the backs of my hands with his thumb, reopening his notebook and adding a tab of highlighter to the nearly finished sketch.

•••

The most effective form of birth control is abstinence. I had to give this speech at least three times daily during my clinical shifts. To my younger patients, I was always tempted to add a second line: *The most effective form of emotional and spiritual protection is abstinence.*

Chris and I had discussed it in the early days of our relationship. It was one of the first things I wanted him to know about me. My friends had always called me a traditional girl: simple, unassuming, except for the one condition I demanded: *If you want me, you have to wait.* I knew myself. I knew I couldn't bear the sting of separation after I had known someone so intimately. I wanted to be both a first and a last. I didn't judge others, nor did I waver in my own choice.

Your boundaries are mine, he'd said. *I'll wait as long as you want.*

It was a learning process. We agreed on one hard boundary. We got too close. We backed away into an awkward no-touch zone where we were afraid to hold hands. We found the affectionate middle ground. True to his word, Chris respected it when he remembered. Sometimes I had to guide his wandering hands, but he always apologized for that.

As a nurse, you remember firsts. You remember the first time you draw blood. The first time you comfort a crying child. The first time you see someone die. The first time you hear a family scream. The first time you watch as a doctor tells someone their time is short. The first time you see a gruesome wound. The first time you see someone fall apart, the first patient whose body you can save while their mind is consumed.

This girl was twenty years old. She was a sophomore at a college down the road from mine, a rising star in the physics department with publications that appeared on the first page of my search engine. Her friends later told hordes of curious reporters that she had always been playful, happy, bubbly. She was a pretty girl, a lively girl, always involved in extracurriculars, next in line to captain the cheer team.

Until one day she finally went insane.

She was complaining of tenderness and bloating in her stomach. The attending physician completed his exam in less than three minutes, barely long enough for me to finish charting on the computer outside her door. When he left the room, he headed straight for me and rolled his eyes.

"Aren't women supposed to *know?*" he sighed, dropping a stack of papers on my table. "Doesn't it feel different? I can't imagine not realizing when you've divided and multiplied."

I blinked. "Excuse me?"

"Ask her if there's any chance she's pregnant. Better know whether it was intentional before we give her the bad news." He shrugged. "I don't see a ring. But who knows what people are up to these days? Offer her counseling, adoption services, the works. A pretty girl like her won't want to be saddled with a kid straight out of school."

What he lacked in empathy, he made up for in speed. He was gone before I could ask any further questions, leaving me to fetch a plastic cup and a test strip.

She looked so small and vulnerable, sitting there with her legs dangling over the end of the examination table, brown hair curling around sweet, red-tinted cheeks. It wouldn't have made any difference how she looked. She glanced up at me as I entered, anxiety in her rapid movement and dilated eyes, and I had a strange thought: *There but for the grace of God go I.*

Pregnancy didn't happen by accident. Pregnancy was a risk no matter how careful you were, which meant that this girl had known what she was doing. A medical professional couldn't spare any pity for mistakes like that. It was just science. Fact. Logic.

"Is there any chance you might be pregnant?" I asked.

She shook her head.

"Would you mind letting us make sure?" I handed her the cup and direct her to the bathroom, a waltz I'd rehearsed a hundred times before. "Just let me know when you're done. I'll run the test. It'll just take a minute."

She departed with a blank expression on her face, clutching the sample cup in both hands as though she desperately needed something to hold onto. A flash of pity jolted me. Perhaps the attending's nonchalance had rubbed off on me. She was routine, after all, a case we saw every day. But it was the first time for her. Not routine for her. Every day I had to remind myself.

I waited outside the bathroom door, tennis shoes tapping the floor. I had an exam the next morning, and I'd been planning to stay up and study. But I was starting to think that no amount of caffeine could keep me out of bed. Maybe there would be time for a cat nap. Maybe I could get up earlier. Maybe I could stop deceiving myself, write off this exam as a lost cause, and start studying earlier next time.

The sample window clinked. My patient had placed the cup inside and closed the door. I pulled on my gloves—difficult with sweaty hands—and reached for the cup.

Empty.

I knocked on the door. "Are you done? Do you need some w—?"

The door flew out from under my knuckles.

A halo of hair. A face full of suffering and anger and panic and hungry, wicked, hunted desperation. Both hands raised, clutched around a little piece of black. Metal and plastic and gunpowder and lead and a tormented mind that meant to send us both to eternity.

The barrel of her gun traced circles in the air. Her hands were shaking—shaking violently, synchronized with her shivers and gasped breaths. An ill-timed twitch of her index finger was all it would take to complete her mission. To end this for both of us—for all three of us, we knew, though I hadn't been able to run the test. The life that lived within her was a testament to her misery. Not a gift. Not a joy. A life forced into her by an evil from the depths of hell.

We understood each other the moment our eyes met, both blurred by terror, both women, both capable of giving life. She was alone and I seemed to have it all together. She had her child, deep inside her, invading the space she had always thought was her own to give and withhold as she pleased. Someone had taken that from her. I had freedom. She had nothing. I had a home to return to. Strong arms to hold me, pull me back up, never force me down. I had love. She had an endless well of wide-eyed, uncomprehending hatred. And she meant for it all to end today.

I raised my hands. One of us had to be in control. One of us had to be unafraid. And I was a nurse, better able to bear the sharp sense of loss and pain than this desperate girl forced to become a woman before she was ready.

"We can help you," I murmured, backing away. There was a call button on the wall behind me. "You have options. You have time. We can—"

"Kill it," she whispered, eyes filling with tears. "Kill me."

Two steps. Two steps more and I'd be there, pressed against the wall.

"You don't have to do this," I babbled. As if that would be enough to distract her. "We don't even know for sure. If you'll just let me run the test, we'll figure out a solution before you leave the hospital. We'll make sure you're taken care of."

"I'd rather die than have his child." Tears streaked unashamedly down her cheeks, leaving rows of glistening salt in her foundation. "If I die, it dies. So please." I shrank away as her weapon wobbled. "I've given you every excuse. Don't make me do this myself."

Another cautious step. One more—one more. I threw myself against the call button, ducking and covering my head with my arms. A code alarm blared. Nurses and doctors came running, pushing a crash cart, prepared for a dying patient but unprepared to witness a supersonic explosion and their colleague's blood on the wall and her body slumped on the floor and my patient kneeling beside her, screaming and crying and begging for her fragile, short life to end.

At least I think that's what happened.

I woke up two days later in a different wing of the hospital, an IV burrowed into my arm, Chris asleep in a recliner beside my bed.

•••

"I don't understand." He hadn't let go of my hand since I woke up, except to use the bathroom and refill my plastic cup of electrolyte water. "Why would she want to kill herself? Why would she shoot you? Why wouldn't she go after the man that did it, or just get an abortion and move on with her life?"

Put so bluntly, it didn't make sense. But I thought I understood. It had something to do with vulnerability. Women were far more willing to acknowledge that than men. We knew we were powerless and desirable, and we walked with the dread that it would be *us next.* That we would be plucked from the vine like a fruit ripe for the taking. That our lives would be forever changed by someone else's vileness.

Taking my life was a choice. Taking her own life would have been her next choice. Dramatic and serious choices with consequences as deep as the choice that had stolen her innocence. One choice for another, traded, an attempt to seize control back from what appeared to be a blind or malicious fate.

Yes. I knew what had made her do it. I wouldn't have done it, but that didn't make me better.

Chris lifted my hand to his lips. "I hope you know I would never hurt you. I hope you always feel secure."

"I do." I did. It had been months since I'd been able to say so honestly. But huddled beneath sterile sheets, blinding white lights raining brilliance on my face, Chris's warmth beside me, my left leg immobilized in a bandage and splint, I felt like I might be invincible. I could get through this. We would never lose control. We would remain the team that had always been fated to make it to the finish line of what a relationship should be.

Maybe this conversation was meant to happen. Maybe this was what we needed to hold together the fragile pieces of us—a reminder of what the world might be like if we didn't have each other.

•••

I discharged myself from the hospital. I filled out the paperwork so my nurse could reapply her smeared mascara for the first time in a twelve-hour shift. Chris watched me work, a slight smile melting the worried wrinkles around his eyes. His hand over mine had never been so gentle.

He pushed my wheelchair to the curb, but instead of engaging the brake while he went to fetch the car, he directed me left, down the paved path to the hospital botanical gardens. I started to protest. I had been dreaming of my own bed and a hot shower—with a garbage bag over my bandaged leg—almost since the moment I'd woken up. But I realized, as the breeze caught my hair, that there was something else I wanted more.

Pain was isolating. Thoughts could be shared, or at least described, but pain had the sinister quality of being purely experiential. You could describe something as aching or throbbing or biting or pounding, which might be specific enough to lead a doctor to a diagnosis, but you would still be the only person to ever experience it. Then there were the nightmares. The girl's face. The hush-hush reports from nurses who were my friends. The whispers. The pitying eyes. Even Chris looked at me that way sometimes, though I had told him to knock it off.

"Please." I twisted my neck, but I still couldn't see much of Chris. "Can we sit for a while?"

"That's where we're headed, sweetheart. Hang in there."

He brought me to a wooden bench surrounded by evergreens, tipped at the edges with melting droplets of frost. Winter hadn't settled in yet, and the breeze lapping my shoulders was easily blocked by Chris's jacket over my shoulders. He helped me angle myself so that my leg was outstretched and my face was in the sun. I sneezed, wiped my nose with the back of my hand, and kissed his cheek.

"Thank you," I whispered, nestling my head into his shoulder as he sat beside me. "Thank you for staying with me."

"It's the least I could do." He returned the kiss on my hair. "I'm glad you're feeling better. I ... when I first got the call, I thought ..."

I'd never heard him hesitate before. Seen his face twist into an expression of total loss, as though the words that had always come so easily had finally dried up.

"You thought?" I prompted gently.

Not that we didn't say we loved each other every time we parted, at random hours in the middle of the day. Not that we didn't hold each other's hands and kiss goodbye. That was a different kind of love than the kind that had been tested by pain and threatened by separation. I wanted Chris to say it. I wanted him to swallow his pride and admit he still loved me—if he did.

Why does it matter so much? I toyed with my own thoughts, trying to tease out the fraying strands of logic. *Is this some kind of test? Do I have any right to test him?*

"I thought," he continued, caressing my hair he had braided down the center of my back, "I've taken you for granted more than I should have. You of all people know how hard it is, balancing medical school with a relationship. I knew you knew, and I thought that made it alright. I made too many excuses for myself these past few months. I want you to know how much you mean to me."

He was right. I'd been doing the same thing—telling myself that our relationship would go back to normal once we were both done with school. Well, here we were, two years into our respective training, and the time we spent together had only dwindled since the first enraptured days. Once upon a time I had thanked God for Chris each night, a giddy little girl enthralled by her first love. Now, to my shame, there were some nights where I only prayed for myself.

"I want you to know there's no one besides you." Chris's hand cupped my elbow, gentle and reassuring. "And I think we should talk about marriage."

It had been two years. It felt like two days. We weren't done with school, but why couldn't we still be committed to each other?

This was undoubtedly what we were supposed to do next.

"What's there to talk about?" It came out too light, too casual. "Of course we're going to get married."

The smile that lit up Chris's face became stamped in my memory. It would put me to sleep at night, wake me up in the mornings, and sometimes keep me awake through the night and bring frustrated, pathetic, angry tears to my eyes for hours after the world around me had gone to sleep.

I never forgot that smile.

•••

Nothing ever happened once with Chris. It wasn't *flowers once* and then never again. It wasn't *I love you* once and then never again. It wasn't an argument once and then never again—a topic, once broached, lingered at the fringes of his consciousness forever.

It wasn't a mistake once and then never again.

I warned him that some mistakes weren't to be repeated. He laughed and made another promise. But inevitably, it happened again. His hands went wandering again. And I had to correct him again, to remind him of the vow in purity we had made two years ago at the beginning of our relationship.

This time, I thought I felt him shrug. I couldn't mistake the sigh.

"Since we're going to be married, I thought— "

"You thought wrong," I said tersely, pushing him away. I was tired of this conversation. Tired of saying *no* only to be asked again. "How could you say that? We're not even engaged yet."

"Is that what I have to do?" he asked playfully. "Then I guess I'd better propose soon."

I stared at him, waiting for him to acknowledge that it was a joke. He sat there, smiling at me. No idea of what he'd said.

Fine. I could spell it out for him, just like I'd done every time before. Except this time, I couldn't bring myself to be gentle. I had always been considerate of his feelings, but I was starting to think he didn't have any. I needed him to prove me wrong.

"Is there anything else you love about me?" I demanded. I didn't try to hide my venom. Honestly, I had always wondered. "Besides my body? Do you want me for anything besides—this?" What was that look in his eyes? "You can't honestly expect me to change my mind now after this has been our normal for two years. You can't think I've changed that much as a person."

"You don't understand how difficult it is, do you?" Bitterness laced his words. "I swore off physical pleasure for you. For two years, I've been faithful in every way you asked. So maybe you can forgive me if I'm running out of patience."

A stab of anxiety rushed through me. I thought we agreed about everything. Values, priorities, goals, sandwich toppings, paint colors on walls, first-line testing methods for Lyme patients. Why was I just now discovering that his agreement with my physical boundaries had been a fantasy—a myth to placate me? Why had I thought it would be so easy to earn his favor?

"A man can't deny himself the way a woman can," Chris continued. As though I wasn't sitting there in frozen shock, legs crossed, hands clasped around ankles, chin tucked to hide the horror I knew must be written on my face. "A man can't wait the way a woman can. I've done everything for you, Lucie, but there's a limit. I can't wait much longer."

"No." I forced a laugh. Why? Why not talk about it now when the subject was fresh? Why did I feel like I had no choice but to deflect, to postpone the inevitable? "No, I suppose not."

His arm descended over my shoulders, and it was all I could do not to shrink—shrink into the bed, through the floor, into the frozen ground of a Franklin winter.

"What kind of ring do you want, pretty girl?"

•••

One day I lost the argument.

I seemed to keep losing it after that.

Day after day, night after night, I was swallowed whole by a sin I never wanted. Not that I disliked it. Not that I would have wanted to wait for anyone else. Not that I hadn't said *yes,* though it felt at the time like it was out of frustration and anger and shame.

Was I the selfish one?

Was it wrong to sacrifice myself for someone else's happiness?

Was a *yes* under pressure the same as the *yes* of love?

Was I allowed to regret it if I liked it?

What was the little goblin that had been gnawing the hole in my chest ever since that first night? Was it guilt? Disgust? Self-hatred? Remorse? Was it God, disappointed in his daughter who had sworn her loyalty only to betray it for a college boyfriend?

Boyfriend.

Because the moment Chris got what he wanted, he seemed to forget about the promise he had given to make me his wife.

Maybe that was just how it went with men. Maybe it was true that they couldn't control themselves the way women could, and that physical urges were more powerful with them. Maybe—maybe—maybe—maybe—

I stood before my mirror, eyes fixed on the sink and ran my brush through tangled hair. Clouds of brown tangled in the bristles. The air was filled with the stale scent of fresh, minty toothpaste and an old bottle of lotion I had nicked from a hotel years ago. The rough skin over my knuckles was cracking. My head ached, and I hadn't slept through the night in weeks. My stomach was tight.

And I knew. Because I was a woman, I knew.

I knew.

•••

I went to work. I wore the same clothes. I masked my nausea with a steady diet of white bread. I made excuses when my jeans wouldn't zip. I broke down and cried in the hospital bathroom. I bought vitamins. I avoided Chris. I avoided everyone, dodging questions with laughter and quips and the bright, sunny smile that came so naturally.

Each morning, I raised my face from the sink and shook the soap off my fingertips, staring at my increasingly haggard reflection, wondering how much concealer it would take to hide the raccoon circles rimming my eyes. *Nursing school,* I said with a laugh. *Really takes it out of ya, huh?* So did not sleeping. So did constant, gnawing, groveling hunger. So did the extra weight and the hormones and the freshly generated blood pounding through my veins at increased pressure. So did uncomprehending, blind terror in the face of the future.

I used to play a morbid game with myself. Who would find out first? Who would be the first to ask the obvious question? It wouldn't be Chris, though he saw me more often than anyone besides my bathroom mirror. He had never been the observant type—he'd missed it when I dyed my hair cherry cola red after its usual deep brown. Maybe it would be my mother, if I managed to conceal my secret until the holidays.

The thought sparked a hole of dread in my stomach. *Mother.* This wasn't what she planned for me. This wasn't the daughter she spoke of with such pride, every time someone left an opening in the conversation. *My favorite nurse* and *my beautiful flower.* I was no longer the little girl she had raised, the daughter of two parents who had waited and planned and carefully protected. I had flirted with womanhood, and it had devoured me.

In the end, the one who found out was my high school best friend.

And that was the bitter, violent, brutal end to everything.

Steven had come to my hospital for a routine procedure. I saw his name in the logs. It had been nearly two years since we'd seen each other in person and almost as long since we'd video called, and that must have accentuated the change in my appearance. He couldn't quite hide the surprise and disappointment in his eyes when I walked into the room. A cynical part of me wondered what he expected a tired, overworked woman to look like. Chris certainly wouldn't know. I never let him find out. I always made myself perfect for him.

"Lucie." The surprise faded, quickly replaced by relief. "I wasn't sure if I should let you know I was here. It's been so long, I thought—"

"I'll take care of this," I told his nurse, twitching the syringe out of her hands before she had a chance to protest. "You wrap up the charting. I'll let you know when I'm done."

Nobody stood on protocol in the hospital's busiest wing. She nodded and scurried off, heading for the computer outside the door. I was left alone with my friend.

My friend.

The one I had been so quick to sacrifice in the name of what I'd once called *love.*

Dense exhaustion overwhelmed me. I didn't know what to tell him. I didn't know where to start. Was there any good way to admit *I made a mistake?* Was there any reason for me to expect that he might understand?

What right did I have to share this burden with him?

"Crickets, Lucie." That had been one of his favorite substitute swear words since we were freshmen, young and fragile and stuck-up in our own knotty morals. "How are you doing?

I had been so desperate for a confidante, I had kept the secret for so long, that I didn't even think. I didn't search for the right words. I didn't hold onto my pride. I didn't think of how it would disrespect Chris. I did complete my task, slipping the medications into his IV—faintly hoping the painkillers would prevent him from remembering that I was ever there—and sat beside him on the hospital bed.

"I'm pregnant," I blurted out. "I think. I haven't taken a test. But I ... I know." It sounded so childish and pathetic. "It's Chris's."

I didn't blame him for the look of revulsion that crossed his face. It only lasted for a second. He was only ashamed of me for a second. Probably he was wondering what had happened to the prim little goody-two-shoes he remembered from high school. He must have also wondered how he ended up in this situation, why I was confiding in him at all. I wondered if he read it as desperation—which it was—or as the sick, silly, sad attempt of an emotional woman to get something for herself.

"What are you going to do?" he asked, when he had control of his face again.

It wasn't an accusation. Just a question.

For some reason, the desperate girl's words echoed in my mind.

Kill it.

Kill me.

I shrugged, shaking off the memory. "I can't have a baby while I'm in nursing school."

"You c—"

"No, Steven. I can't." Did he think I hadn't already considered all the options? Did he think I, a medical professional, didn't know? "It's not what you think. It's horrible. I've already had to call out of work multiple times for morning sickness. My back hurts. Everything hurts. The health risks ... the time it would take to care for the baby ... the ..." *Shame. Stares. Pity. Judgment.* "I have to finish school first. Get married. Settle down. Think about whether this is really what I want. I'm not cut out to be a mother anyway. You of all people should remember how much I hated babysitting your younger siblings when you had hockey matches. I'm not gentle. I'm not even nice. I wouldn't trust myself to raise a child."

"Oh, please. You'd be a great mother." He sat up straighter, wincing as his bandages pulled tight. "And you could still finish school. Worst comes to worst, your parents would probably help you figure out childcare. They don't live far away, and they love grandbabies. You know they mention it pretty much every time you're home."

He didn't get it. I didn't blame him, since this wasn't a situation he could even dream of facing. It's not *right.* It wasn't supposed to be like *this.* I wasn't supposed to turn out *this way.* For nine months and then forever, I would be forced to preserve and protect my own scarlet letter. The child into which I was supposed to pour endless love and devotion would be the permanent souvenir of the mistakes I'd made.

It was a matter of conscience. I couldn't bring a child into the world only to brand her as something that was never meant to be.

I would never tell Chris. Nor my parents. Not anyone. I would let the burden of this secret be mine and God's for all eternity.

This would be the lesser weight of guilt.

"Lucie." Steven's laugh was shaky. "Do you need a hug?"

"Yes." I sank into his arms, biting my tongue to hold back the tears. "I'm sorry, Steven. I know this isn't what you came here for. I didn't mean to tell you, but—"

"We're friends, Lucie." He gave me a squeeze. "This is what friends do. They listen. They care."

Through the glass panel in the door I saw him standing there, arms crossed over his chest. His face was so twisted in anger that I barely recognized it at first. And when I did, I shivered.

I didn't know what I had done, but I could tell from his look that I was going to pay for it.

Chris, please—

I promise I still love you.

•••

"I can explain. I swear. He was in the hospital for a procedure, and I—"

"So, you sat on the bed with him."

Chris was dragging me across the parking lot, weaving between cars toward our favorite taco restaurant. He'd promised to take me tonight, and he was keeping that promise so violently that my right shoulder ached and my tennis shoes were skidding across the frosty ground.

"You sat on the bed with him," he repeated with a vicious yank of my hand, "and you let him hug you like that. What were you talking about, Lucie? Tell me. What were you talking about that you had to get so close?"

I couldn't answer. I *couldn't.* He'd understand if he knew—but he couldn't know. Once he knew, he'd feel the guilt too. He was too good of a man not to feel it. And this burden was mine—mine alone—mine to carry.

But I couldn't lie to Chris. My love. My soon-to-be fiancé. I did the worst possible thing and I said, looking at his back: "I can't tell you."

"Tell me."

"I can't."

"Tell me!" It came out in a shout as he turned around, forcing me onto the sidewalk with him. His face was so close that I could smell his breath, fresh and relentlessly minty. Because Chris had it all together. Chris was always well-kempt and perfect. I was the rotten one, the one who was lucky to have anyone at all.

"Tell me what you did," he hissed, pulling me close, "or I'll assume the worst."

I opened my mouth. I had no idea what to say. Words swirled around my mind, blending and mixing and getting hopelessly tangled in long, meaningless strings of sound. I was paralyzed. Overwhelmed. Scared. I had never once been scared of Chris. Not that I really thought he would hurt me, but we had never fought so close before, so physically and emotionally and publicly. My face grew hot with embarrassment as I pictured what the diners in the restaurant must be thinking. Probably they were looking out the window, murmuring in low voices about how *we should all know less about each other, why does she let him treat her like that? Why doesn't she just walk away? Why does she love him? Why doesn't she just say "no?"*

Real life is never that simple, my soul cried, but no one was listening. No one saw the silent tears that formed in the corners of my eyes, the trembling lips I turned upward to give Chris the smallest of smiles.

"I love you," I whispered shakily, hoping he would see that I meant it. How could he mistake my sincerity? After all this time, after all we'd been through, after two years together, how could he think I was lying? "I can't tell you what Steven and I were talking about. It's a surprise. I'll tell you later."

"A surprise."

Really, the only surprise was the dryness in his voice and the shock that swelled up inside me as he said it. He didn't believe me. He didn't even pity me. The man who had dried so many of my tears, who had comforted me so many times, who was moved almost to tears himself by my sniffles, had lost the ability to discern between love and lies.

Is it really so unfair for him to demand proof?

It's not even proof he wants. It's just an explanation.

Why would you offer him your word when you could just explain?

I took a deep breath, trying to settle my racing heart.

"I don't know how to tell you this," I began, my voice low, my chin tucked, my heart ashamed. "I ... I wasn't going to tell you, but—"

Maybe it shouldn't have come as a surprise.

Maybe I should have seen it coming.

Maybe there had been plenty of warnings.

Christophe was a forceful man, a take-charge-when-it-mattered kind of man.

This will never happen again.

How could you ask for anything else from me?

Is that what I have to do?

In any case, his backhand to my face surprised me.

As did the next one.

And the next.

And history repeated itself. The one with power above me. The sky above, watching with lurid brightness the crimes committed under its canopy. The ground rose up like a cradle to hold me, to force me to sink no further in my feeble attempt to protect myself and—for some reason—the little life inside me, which for one primal moment seemed like the most important thing in the world.

My ears rang. My mouth filled with iron. *Pop* and *crack* and *"How could you do this to me? How could you? Did you think I'd let you get away with it?"* and sirens and bustle and crowds and onlookers and shame and guilt and pain and pain, so much pain, enough pain to fill my body and my child's body, and the familiar reek of blood and boots around me and uniform pants and sirens, more sirens, and wild, incomprehensible screams of rage and pain and fear.

•••

She has a kind face.

That was the only thought I could piece together from the confused mush of colors and shapes. At least I knew where I was, and that was somewhere familiar. I had been an EMT before I was a nurse, and the antiseptic scent of a clean-scrubbed rig felt like homesickness. I should never have left.

"Chris." Why wouldn't my lips work? Why were they sticking together? What was that awful, dry, lurid taste in my mouth. "Where's Chris?"

The EMT on the bench beside me glanced up at her partner. Concern was written all over her face, and I knew that look. I'd looked at my attending that way when a patient asked me a question I knew would be agony to answer.

"Where's Chris?" I demanded.

"You won't be seeing that man again for a long time," the EMT said at last. Her partner was busy with charting—or so I guessed from the overly loud and jarring chirp of a laptop keyboard from behind my head.

"And sweetheart." She paused. "I think that's a good thing."

•••

No doctor takes a crying patient seriously. Everyone cries in a hospital—the nurses, the residents, the doctors, the janitors who clean the blood from the floor. They only train you to give the bad news, not the good, because there's so seldom anything else to give.

They wouldn't let me see the scans until I stopped crying. And then they wouldn't believe that I'd stopped crying until my eyes dried. They wouldn't let me have a sip of water because I was crying so hard they thought I'd choke, and they wouldn't give me painkillers for the subsequent headache because they thought I wanted to drift away and leave them, leave my child, leave Chris, leave everyone. They put a teal band around my wrist so that everyone knew the extent of my shame.

This one must be watched.

This one is a danger to herself.

I was. I had judged others and *there without the grace of God, went I.*

Without.

Grace.

I had always wondered what it would be like to truly be alone. To stand in an empty room and watch my own soul, bare, reflected in the surface of a silent, brooding, lonely glass. I never believed it was possible to get so far outside myself that I could look back in through my own eyes, staring into the depths of my mind and laying bare the thoughts and secrets my heart held close. But it turned out that pain could do that. Suffering showed you who you were and held you by the throat until you accepted it.

I would never accept this. I would never accept myself. I would never accept the changes in my body, the thinning hair, the dry skin, the headaches, the sickness, the rounded stomach. I would never accept what they meant. I would never accept that Chris was gone.

At first, I begged to see him. I endured the curious stares of my colleagues, the ones who were privy to my chart or to the gossip chain and knew that security had orders to remove him from the hospital on sight. I pleaded and prayed and cried and reminded them of past favors I had done—wrapping up a chart, fetching a vial, calming a difficult patient. *I would do the same for you,* I reminded them. It wasn't until one of the nurses grew huffy and exclaimed: "Of course you wouldn't be so foolish!" that I stopped.

I stopped speaking to anyone after that.

Life grew inside me.

Adoption and abortion counselors drifted in and out of my room, leaving a growing mound of pamphlets on my bedside table. When the trauma cart rushed by in the hallway, some of them would fall, scattering like flies around the room until the mealtime nurse reorganized them. Photographs of babies, of smiling women and families and children and crosses and churches and doctors and nitrile gloves littered every spare surface. Oxygen hissed. Monitors beeped. Sterile fluid dripped into my veins. Night went and morning came and I lost all sense of time, dozing in and out, grounded only by the clicking of tennis shoes back and forth in the hallway.

"What are you going to do?"

The young doctor stood by the foot of my bed. Somewhere, someone had written in my chart that men were not to get too close. I knew the protocol with assaults.

It wasn't an assault. It was an argument, that's all.

I tucked my chin into my blanket, defiant.

"What are you going to do?" he repeated. "You can't stay here forever, Lucie. You have to go home. You'd feel more comfortable there, wouldn't you? And you'd have time to get ready for the baby, if you ... depending on what you decide."

Decide.

My whole chest ached. Every future decision had been stolen from me by the one I had made three months earlier in response to Chris's urging. There was nothing left to decide. Nothing important. The *when* and the *how* and the *where* of death were only minor details in a story that had been written since the beginning of time.

Was this how I was supposed to turn out? Had this always been the plan for me?

Did You know this was going to happen?

"Lucie?" the doctor prompted.

There it was in his eyes, too—the emotion I had come to hate.

"No," I snarled, pulling the blanket tightly over my face. "I don't want to go home. I can't go home."

My parents were the only ones who still didn't know. The only ones who still had a memory of their daughter the way she was before—this. I couldn't tell them what I had become. Not until I had the situation under control.

Not until the irreversible was done.

"Schedule me for the procedure." I rolled over and clutched my pillow to my chest. "As soon as possible. You're right. I want to go home."

"Lucie." Distress laced the doctor's voice, and it almost got me to look up.

I hid the beginnings of tears in the limp hospital pillow.

"Are you ... are you sure?" The words came slowly. He knew it wasn't his place.

I would have hit him if I could reach him. Because I wasn't sure. Despite what I had told Steven, laughing off his kindness, I knew myself. I was a nurse—a paid mother for the unfortunate and the lonely. I loved it. I was good at it. I couldn't imagine the love I would feel for a child, a feeble life of my own.

But half that life was Chris. And Chris was the vicious, violent, hateful past. If they forced me to move on from him, I would. I'd move on altogether. Without Chris, without our marriage, without our love, alone, I could never care for a child any more than I could care for myself when I came down with the campus flu.

I'd heard it said before: *The timing just wasn't right.* How simple it sounded then, as if the only thing standing in the way of happiness was the brittle hands of a clock.

"I'm sure," I told the doctor, turning over in the bed. "I want this to be over."

•••

I braid my hair and loop it in a crown over my head. I choose my softest cardigan, my biggest sweatpants that fit tight over my rounded belly. I remove my earrings and my necklace. I don't apply makeup.

I'm ready.

My body aches, and I pull my coat tightly around my chest. Winter has turned bitter, and the breeze nips at the dry skin on my cheeks. I feel strangely vulnerable, scurrying down the sidewalk, pushing my way between students on their way to class. As if they can all see where I'm going, where I came from. What I'm about to do.

I know the medical truth about abortion. I've seen pictures of it in my classes. I've counseled women before and after the procedure, and I've seen the emptiness in their faces when they describe it. The truth is, abortion is almost always a last resort. It's not just another form of birth control. It's an invasion of the woman's body, a violent wrenching apart of the wounds inside her.

Desperation drives me, and I feel anything but free. I feel as if Chris is the one holding the forceps. As if he'll be waiting at the clinic.

He isn't. I pass by the line of protesters, my eyes fixed firmly on the sidewalk. They don't know. They'll return to their cozy homes and kiss their spouses. Play with their kids, make them dinner, put them to bed. They think that just because they were lucky enough to hold it together, everyone else can do the same. They don't know what it means to be truly out of options. To be ashamed, alone. To know without asking that even God feels his cheeks burn when he looks your way.

"Are you sure you want this?" Someone grabs my arm. "There are other options, you know. Adoption could—"

"Do you know how horrible the adoption system is?" I snarl, wrenching my arm free. "Do you know what happens to those kids? I wouldn't wish that on my worst enemy, let alone my child."

"So, you're going to kill it?" Another shrill voice rises above the clamor, and I shrink back. "Become a murderer? Is that what you want?"

The tears in the corners of my eyes sting so fiercely that I wonder if they're already freezing. "Leave me alone. I don't want this any more than you do."

I never wanted any of this. I had said *no* more times than I could count. I used to love teasing Chris, provoking him, flirting with him in the security and loveliness of my womanhood. I had stopped when I realized that he couldn't help himself. I had avoided touching him, covered myself carefully, avoided offering any temptation that I knew might drive him over the edge. I guess it turned out that I was never the problem—until I stayed with him when he refused to accept my *no.*

"Do you really want this to be your child's last day on earth?" someone yells.

I flinch. Snow slips under my boot, and I fall into the arms of a pretty redheaded woman. The fringe on her scarf brushes my hands, warm and soft, and that's all it takes for the tears to spill down my cheeks.

She sets me on my feet and helps me dust off the snow on my jeans.

"That was close," she says, smiling. There's a kindness in the crinkle of her eyes that, for some reason, brings fresh tears. "Do you like spaghetti?"

•••

I'm slurping noodles with a stranger, looking at pictures of her cat on a phone screen tinted green from the cold. It's awkward at first. We talk about the weather and about my classes at school. She doesn't ask me what happened, and I'm grateful for the chance to think about anything else.

The windows are wrapped by cold, gray skies. Snow blurs the street, gradually heaping over the curb until the sidewalk is indistinguishable from the road. Day students in heavy coats trample paths through the white, faces anonymized by their scarves. It's getting dark. I'm on my third glass of water.

"So, tell me." Carrie is her name, I think, though she only said it once and I'm afraid to admit I wasn't paying attention. "How far along are you?"

I don't know what I was thinking, letting myself believe we were friends. Of course she wanted something from me. A promise. A conversion. Little does she know, I'm already converted. I mumble an answer and pick at my food.

"Is the father in the picture?" she presses.

"He doesn't know." Thank God. I fear what he'd do to me if he found out about my secret. "He was abusive. Not ... not all the time. Just once. At the end."

Carrie clicks her tongue. "Once is one too many."

"That's what they say." I hate myself. That's what I would say to any of my friends if they asked for my advice. Why is it so hard to believe it myself?

"You'd be alone, caring for the child," she continues when the silence gets awkward. "I can see why that would be intimidating."

Intimidating. What an odd choice of words. As if birthing and raising a child is little more than a hill that looks too steep to climb.

"I'd have to bring my child to class. Everyone would know." My words choke. "I'd have to tell my parents. I'd have to get another job. Move out of the dorms. Pay rent and utilities for an apartment. Take care of a child instead of studying. Lose sleep—I already don't sleep. Never sleep. If Chris finds out, I might have to share custody. I don't even know how that works. I can't take care of a child when I can barely take care of myself. One of us ... one of us would end up getting themselves killed."

"I'm not trying to convince you to keep the child," she says. "I'm trying to convince you of what you're doing. What will happen if you reschedule that appointment."

"You think you know more about it than me?" At first, I bristle, but regret hits immediately. "This isn't a complicated procedure. I know exactly how it works. I don't need you to tell me."

"How much do you know about what happens after?"

"What do you mean?"

"Do you think you'll grieve the child?"

I've considered it. I've been trying not to. Yes, most women grieve their unborn children, if only because of what might have been. Abortion is almost always a last resort. Of course, we would all prefer to have happy families, to have room for new life. But sometimes life isn't so gentle.

"Of course." My noodles have long gone cold, but I take another bite anyway. "I thought I was going to marry the father. It's not just the child I'll be grieving." And God only knows when that sting will disappear—if it ever does. I could swear I still feel Chris's hands on my face sometimes, cupped around my jaw, striking my cheek.

She pushes a waterfall of gold-tinted hair behind her ear, staring down at her plate. "What would you grieve if you had the child?"

"Excuse me?"

"It's a serious question. You'll lose something either way. What would you be grieving if you carried the child to term?"

The list is so long I hardly know where to start. My family's pride. My own pride, I think, and my ability to face my own reflection in the mirror. My time. My friends. My career. The perfect romance I'd always dreamed of. Chris. Always Chris. I wonder if the child would have his eyes, and at what age I would see them for the first time.

"Do you value all that as much as you value her life? Supposing it's a little girl, of course." Carrie smiles, and there's a little ruefulness in her laughter. "I'm sorry. I have a girl at home. She's two now."

"Oh." I wonder why she didn't show me pictures of her daughter. "But it's not a life. Not yet. It's just a ... an idea of what might have been."

"It is a life. It's there, inside you. Just not quite in the way we usually know it." She pauses. "Do you always give up on your dreams so easily?"

I choke on my noodles.

"'What might have been,' you said. Why can't it be?" she insists. "With a little help, why can't that future be yours?"

"I ... because ..."

"You'll lose friends over this. You might fight with your family. Of course you'll have to make sacrifices, and of course it will never be as simple as it would have been to do it all on your own. But isn't life more valuable than all that?"

"Life. *If* it's life."

"Is she alive? This baby of yours—is she alive right now?"

"Of course *it's* alive." I hug my arms around my chest. "It's made of cells. But that doesn't make it human. And if you think I have a problem killing a bunch of cells—"

"Is that what a stillbirth is? A miscarriage? Is that simply a loss of cells?"

"No, but that's later in the—"

"What do you feel is growing inside you right now?" She's leaning across the table now, brown eyes peering gently into mine. She really believes this, I conclude with an uncomfortable sense of shock. "Is it cells? Or is it life?"

Why does it matter what I feel? I feel as if I'm cold when I have a fever. I feel hungry when I've already eaten. I feel as though an offspring of Chris has taken up residence inside my body, rotting my insides and stealing the nourishment from my heart, body, and soul. What I feel isn't always right.

I feel as though my body is a warm, safe place. I feel as though the child's soul is innocent of her father's crimes. I feel that I could be a good mother, gentle and loving and caring, self-sacrificing for the most perfect cause. I feel that my daughter and I could endure all the stares, all the judgment, all the pity. I feel that we could do it together, with the help of the God who created us both.

God.

Will God forgive me for this?

Maybe, I realize with a shiver, God is the only one who will.

If I have to live with the results of my sin for the rest of my life, what will God see when He looks at me? Will he see Chris's child or mine? A life redeemed or a life recklessly wasted? Happiness after all, or suffering extended years beyond the fatal choice was made?

Water drips in my spaghetti. I blink, surprised, and find that I've been crying.

Carrie holds her arms open, and I shove the spaghetti and my pride out of the way, falling across the table into her embrace. The smell of her laundry detergent fills my nose, sweet and crisp and unfamiliar. Her hair is rough and thick. I don't know this woman. I don't know anything about her, besides that she has an orange cat and a two-year-old daughter and hates the cold, but maybe after all we do have something in common. Maybe we both want the same thing: nurture, love, and fulfillment for the least of these.

•••

It's a different kind of love. It's exhaustion and sacrifice. It's delight and warmth and companionship and unconditional, eternal, infinite grace. I understand now how God can forgive any repentant sinner. If imperfect, exhausted Lucie can do this for her daughter, how much more can He do for His?

She doesn't have her dad's eyes. She doesn't have mine, either. She has her own, pale green orbs framed by long, perfect eyelashes. She can bat them from across the room and have me running to do her bidding.

I moved home, planning to finish nursing school online. "No one cares how you do it," one of my professors told me, "so long as you do it." So I do. I'm not completely alone. During exams, during clinical shifts and moments of weakness, my family helps out. They were brokenhearted at first, nearly as much as I was, but we all soon realized that "mistake" is a temporary word. "Redemption" is permanent.

Little Carrie grips my leg, laughing and playing with the flowers embroidered on my jeans. A haggard Steven makes a dive for her, trying to shoo her away from "Mommy's workspace." I laugh. Of course she has no idea what the word means, and she just wants our combined attention. That used to bother me, but never very much. I've learned to do my focused work after she's in bed.

"Thanks for the help," I tell Steven. Carrie squeaks in delight as he picks her up. "She's got some energy today. Are you sure she didn't sneak a sip from your coffee earlier?"

There are dark circles under his eyes, but he grins as he bounces Carrie. "I might have given her a sip of the mocha."

He already promised to watch her for the rest of the afternoon while I study for my board exam. He'll have to help her burn off the excess energy. And I'll watch, peeking over the back of my computer when the lecture comes to a place I already know by heart, hiding my smile behind my notes as Steven lets himself be tackled by the little girl in a princess dress.

I can only imagine my life the way it is now. I can't think of anything else.

It took longer than I expected. Everything did. It was harder in many ways, easier in others. But there's a kind of hopefulness in leaving the past behind me, letting the old fade away. I never would have accepted this adventure before, but I'm a different person now. Carrie is different than her parents. Steven is different than me. Everyone is different in the ways that matter. And reminders of the past are just that—reminders. Not the past itself. Not the experiences, the memories. Simply little relics that let me know: *I survived.*

She does have his eyes, if I'm being honest. The same light brown and soft green flecks. They are my greatest hope for the future. Because when I look into them, I don't see anger. I don't see rage or hatred or pain. I see love, a gentle spirit, an uncorrupted nature that I have the privilege of cherishing. I see that the past made the present but failed to define it. I see a horrible thing turned beautiful by the power of the One who promised I would survive if I only trusted His plan.

Carrie's laughter pulls me out of my thoughts. She's riding Steven's shoulders now, waving a bejeweled fairy wand around his head, ordering him to take her to the ball so she can show off her new feather boa. Her words are incomprehensible through her delight, but the meaning is clear enough as she tugs the clasp of Steven's necklace like reins.

Maybe I was wrong about love. Maybe it's not something big, something small, something perfect or delicate. Maybe love holds a sword, conquering the evil in its path and sweetly bending it to the service of the good. Maybe love is a suit of armor without a crack, smooth and unblemished and formed in the perfect image of what it means to be a human with an eternal soul.

Maybe love is infinite. Maybe love is a Person, and it's divine.

Lauren Smyth is a journalist, freelance editor, and lover of all things adventurous. Her most recent novel is *Warsafe* (Enclave Publishing, 2025). Since signing her first publishing contract at age 13, she has written three young adult novels, coded two narrative video games, and started a blog enjoyed by readers and writers around the world. Her books, writing podcast, newsletter, and more can be found at **https://www.laurensmythbooks.com**

THE LIFE TO SAVE
BY JOANNA WHITE

"I can't believe you're home!" Mia laugh-cried as she darted up to embrace her fiancé, Rhett Callum, who had just walked in the door after being deployed for almost a year. As his strong arms came around her and she wrapped hers around his waist, she breathed in his scent of sandalwood and the outdoors. For a long moment, they just stood in their embrace, and Mia tried to tell herself that he was *real*.

Sometimes, she had dreamed about him being back and would wake to realize he wasn't. Other times, in that glorious moment between sleep and waking, she would still feel like he stood in the room with her ... until she fully woke and reality hit. Those moments always crushed her the most.

Rhett's thick brown beard, likely from not shaving overseas while on his deployment, tickled her cheek as he pressed his face against hers. His hair looked lighter after being out in the sun especially compared to her dark wavy locks. His head sank onto her shoulder as he groaned deep in his chest, a rumble that made her laugh. "I've missed you so much, Mia."

"I've missed you more than words." Mia sniffled, trying to calm the tracks of tears making their way down her cheeks, but she couldn't stop them, couldn't help the emotion at the sight of her fiancé. "But your deployment isn't over yet ... I didn't think you'd come back in time for Thanksgiving, let alone on Thanksgiving Day! How?"

Rhett smiled. "We had a leave block scheduled, so a group of us got to come home. I'll be here for three weeks."

"Three weeks?" Mia laugh-cried again and kept running her hands along his toned arms. It meant he would leave just before Christmas, but he was home now, which was all that mattered.

Rhett nodded. He looked more worn than when she saw him last; his usual ivory skin was tanned and almost leathery from obvious days in the sun. And he had a new scar over his left eyebrow that angled down toward his eye. She admired the beard on his rectangular jaw as she searched him for any other new scars or obvious wounds. Part of her wondered where he had been sent to; as a Navy SEAL, he could never tell her where.

"I'm alright, *mi corazón,*" he murmured in Spanish as if he knew she had been looking him over for injuries.

At that, she smiled. When they had first met, he had jokingly teased her about her name.

"Mia? As in 'mi corazón'?"

Mia laughed. "I'm not Mexican or from Spain or anything, so no. Just an American gal, born and bred." At that, she chuckled. "You're also not as funny as you think you are."

Rhett shrugged. "But you laughed."

"Fair enough." Mia shook her head at him and playfully rolled her eyes.

"Mi corazón ... I like it." Rhett flashed her a handsome grin. "It's about all I remember from my high school Spanish."

Ever since then, the nickname stuck and eventually became a term of endearment as their relationship had grown more serious.

"Am I that obvious?" she asked as she gazed up at his soft blue eyes.

Rhett held up his index finger and thumb. "Little bit."

She opened the door to her tiny apartment wider with a sigh. "Sorry about the heat." Their state stayed hotter than it should have been this time of year. She pursed her lips, not wanting to admit that her utilities had been shut off. In truth, she hadn't even told either of her parents. She hadn't told her mom, Elaine, because she'd insist on helping pay for it, and Mia didn't want to do that to her mom. And she certainly hadn't told her father, Travis, because it would prove he'd been right that Mia's singing career wasn't a career and she should follow in his family business and "make something of herself."

Rhett frowned as he stepped in, and her hopes fell that the windows would provide enough light that he wouldn't notice the lack of electricity. "Mia, what's going on?"

"What do you mean? You know what, your parents invited Mom and I over for dinner for Thanksgiving tonight. They'll be so excited to have you. Do you think they'll still be okay with Mom and I coming or would they want Thanksgiving alone with you since you're here? I'll cook. It'd give your mom a break." Mia took his hand and pushed him closer to the door.

Rhett frowned and gently snatched her shoulders. "Mia, stop deflecting. I'm trained. You're not gonna fool me. Now tell me what's going on."

Mia chewed on her lower lip. "Um, well ..."

"Did your utilities get shut off?" Rhett released her with a frown.

Mia rubbed the back of her neck as her cheeks heated. "I just ... Rent's been so expensive, and these local gigs barely pay enough for that and food, so some things have had to ... go." Thank goodness she was on her mom's phone plan; if not, a phone would have been the first to go. At the moment, Mia refused to let Elaine pay for anything other than their phones.

Rhett shook his head, crossing his arms over his muscled chest. "No, I'm not gonna let you live like this."

Mia exhaled sharply. "I don't want to beg my dad for money for the wedding, and I've been trying to save, but ..." Her voice trailed off.

Rhett took her in his arms and gently tugged her against his chest again. "I'll pay for the wedding, *mi corazón.* Why don't we head over to my house for dinner, and then we'll come back and go over the finances, okay?"

"But ... are you sure?" Mia bit her lip again.

Rhett gently tilted her head up to look at him. "You're going to be my wife. It's my job to protect and provide for you. And I want to support your dream; I want you to be able to live your dream and the calling God's given you."

Mia wiped tears from her eyes and hid herself against him. He had no idea how much it meant to her, to have a man support and protect her the way her father should have. To know that Rhett wanted her to dream and follow God's calling, that he believed in her when her father never had ...

She sniffled. "Thank you. You know how much I love you, right, Rhett?"

Rhett nodded. "Oh, I know." But his smile said it all.

"I do hope you get something out of this relationship," Mia muttered.

Rhett slung his arm around her shoulders affectionately, and she fit perfectly beneath his arm as they headed to the door. "I do, trust me, *mi corazón.*"

Mia turned around and locked her door—not that she had anything worth stealing besides her guitar she'd bought at sixteen after saving up for four years—but when she started toward her beat-up old Jeep Wrangler, Rhett steered her the other way to his white Chevy.

"Speaking of God's calling and our passions ..." She swallowed and gathered the courage to get the words out. "Um, how long until your service ends?"

Rhett gazed down at her, and his eyes softened. "I've still got several more years yet, Mi. And when I go back, I'll have to finish out the rest of the deployment." He opened up the passenger door for her and helped boost her into the seat since her short, petite frame struggled to get in. "I know this life is difficult. I don't want you to marry me and end up regretting anything. If you wanna back out ..." Rhett glared at the ground.

"Hey! Of course I don't want to back out." Mia reached out and grasped his hand, giving it a reassuring squeeze. "I love you, and you're stuck with me for life, Rhett Callum."

2

Thanksgiving dinner with his parents and her mom had been wonderful. She had visited them a few times during his deployment, but it always felt like she had imposed herself on them whenever she visited without him. His mom, Donna Callum, always seemed happy to see Mia, and she had a feeling Mia reminded her of Rhett when he had been gone. On top of that, she wasn't one of those overbearing mother-in-laws who tried to butt in during wedding stuff. Mia's older sister had married into another rich family in town, thanks to their father, and her mother-in-law had controlled *everything*. It worried Mia, but she felt more at ease every time she met up with Donna. Besides, Donna and Elaine had become good friends, which warmed Mia's heart.

The day after he got back, while everyone else went Black Friday shopping, Mia and Rhett dove right into wedding planning. Or, rather, Mia did. Rhett insisted he didn't care and that he just wanted her to be happy. They had both been active in their local church—and both still were—so they had already spoken to the pastor and let him know Rhett had come back. Everything seemed to be going perfectly in planning their wedding and life together. Putting it together in three weeks would be fast, but Rhett and Mia both wanted to marry before he shipped back out.

Rhett understood Mia's need to provide for herself, even though she knew she'd have to get used to the idea of Rhett taking care of her financially. As an active-duty Navy SEAL, he earned enough to help them both. On Sunday night, he had helped her find another gig after church and watched the whole thing to support her. The payment would help her finally pay her bills so she could get her utilities turned back on.

After the gig, they came back to Rhett's house. He'd bought it and moved out of his parents' shortly after he graduated high school. He'd worked and saved up a ton of money, which Mia discovered he was exceptionally good at. His parents had kept up with it in the time he'd been gone.

"Wow. Not even a speck of dust in here." Rhett laughed as he slung his arm around her.

"Your mother is nothing if not a perfectionist. I came and helped her clean the place a few times. Not that a one-bedroom house needed much cleaning." Mia laughed and spun them around. "Ah, that gig went so well! The crowd really loved it. And church today was great."

Rhett nodded and planted a kiss on her forehead as he wrapped his arms around her while they swayed like they were dancing even though they didn't have any music playing. "Yeah, and it's good that the coffee shop let you sing for music night. Last time I was here, you had issues with them letting you sing at any of their events because they were 'concerned' that your Christian music would 'offend' someone."

Mia snorted. "Yeah. Like anyone in this small town is gonna be offended. Everyone here either goes to our church or the Catholic one, so ... I'm just glad I'm not dealing with that anymore. But hey, Trinity caught me in the bathroom afterward, and she asked if I could sing at her wedding reception at the end of the start of next year."

Rhett grinned as the two plopped down onto his loveseat. "I'm glad. One of my other buddies, Nate, is planning on getting married when this deployment ends, probably next spring, so I can talk to him when I meet his fiancé. Maybe you'll get to sing at their wedding."

Mia sighed and snuggled up against his side. "I'd like that. I thought about singing at ours, but that'd be too cheesy, right?"

Rhett gently tapped her nose. "You can serenade me all you want. You have the voice of an angel."

Mia rolled her eyes. "You're biased."

Rhett planted a soft kiss on her lips. "No, just in love."

Mia chuckled. "Okay, now that's cheesy." Her eyes trailed down his arms. Now that he wore a snuggly fit tee shirt and gym shorts, she saw several new scars on his arms and his legs. Each one made her wonder what happened, but part of her wasn't sure she should ask.

"Now ..." Mia cleared her throat and gestured to his phone. "You have to turn that true crime podcast back on. The drive home wasn't long enough to finish it, and you can't leave me wondering what happened."

Rhett smirked at her and scrolled on his phone to open the podcast. "Are you telling me that you're *actually* getting into true crime podcasts now?"

Mia's cheeks heated, and she smiled so hard her cheeks hurt. "Maaayybe." She drew it out with a giggle.

Rhett rolled his blue eyes that looked brighter in the stark white lighting of his small, one-bedroom house. No part of the house looked personal; he hadn't hung anything on the walls, and aside from the basic loveseat, small TV, single bookshelf full of mysteries, and a bed in the other room, it hardly seemed like a *home.* But Rhett told her he didn't see the point since they planned to move into the house he was building for them. "We'll make that our home," he always used to say. "Maybe, huh? You know, one of these days, I'm gonna make you a fan of the dark and mysterious—teach you to embrace one of my greatest passions."

Mia shook her head. "I'll never understand why horrible crimes and dark mysteries fascinate you."

Rhett shrugged. "They *relax* me."

Mia scoffed. "You're insane if they relax you. It literally makes no sense."

"Are you judging me?" Rhett quirked an eyebrow at her.

Mia planted a kiss on his cheek, and his beard tickled her. "Maaaybe."

"That's your word of the day, you know." Rhett turned on the podcast, and as they listened to the rest of the crime, he pulled out his computer.

"Have you written anything?" Mia murmured.

Rhett shook his head. "Nope. I haven't had much inspiration. Then again, I've been deployed for a year so ..."

Mia settled herself against him and wrapped her arms around his waist. "Maybe this true crime podcast will help you get your inspiration back. And as soon as you finish writing that mystery of yours, I want to read it."

Rhett's cheeks ... reddened. "Maaaybe." He flashed her a wide grin.

Mia chortled so hard she couldn't breathe. "Are you actually *blushing*, big bad soldier?"

"No!" Rhett laughed. The two giggled and settled in to finish listening to the podcast. That night, he was reluctant to take her home without her utilities on yet, so he offered to let her stay with him. "Rhett, I got paid tonight. I'll get them back on in the morning."

"Nonsense," Rhett said. He let her take his bed, and he slept on the couch. Now that he had come home, she wanted to spend every moment with him that she could, so she didn't argue.

"Hey, tomorrow, we can look for decorations for the new house," Rhett said.

"That sounds fun to me! Goodnight."

"Night, *mi corazón.*" Rhett flipped off his light and left his room so she could get some sleep.

The next morning, after eating breakfast at a café, Mia paid her utility bill, and they headed back over to her house and hung out the rest of the day. That night, Rhett and Mia sat on the couch together, flipping through different house decorations on their phones.

"Oh, look at this one!" Mia gushed.

Rhett peeked over at her phone. "Yeah, I really like that. We could use the extra bedroom as a music room for you."

Mia giggled. "That would be so exciting."

He had always been passionate about renovating, and even though Mia felt her calling had always been in music and singing, she enjoyed decorating. He had started to fix up a house for them out in the country just outside of town, but it wasn't anywhere near livable yet. The two planned to work on it more together the closer to the wedding. But they both had fun saving ideas and dreaming.

Rhett's phone rang. When he looked at the caller, his expression sobered. "This is Callum."

Mia's heart sped up, and she stared at him. He had used his work voice, and the thought terrified her.

Rhett's eyebrows furrowed as he nodded. "I understand, sir."

No. Tears filled Mia's eyes, and she blinked, trying not to shed them. Maybe it wouldn't be—

"I'll head over to base at zero-eight-hundred tomorrow morning." Rhett paused. "Yes, sir."

Mia squeezed her eyes closed. *God, please let him just have to go to the base and work. Please don't let it—*

Rhett released a slow, deep breath. "Mia."

She opened her eyes and didn't want to see what she saw in his pained gaze. "No. No, don't you dare tell me what I think you're gonna say, Rhett Callum!" The tears finally spilled over. "Y–you're supposed to have three weeks for the holiday."

"I'm being called out again, Mia. They're cutting it early. I'm *so sorry.*" Rhett's voice sounded strained as he reached out for her.

Mia wiped furiously at her burning eyes. "For how long?"

"I don't know. I don't even know where I'm going yet." Rhett grasped her hands, but as she tried to pull away, he kept ahold of her and refused to release her. "Mia, I'm *sorry.* But I have to go."

Mia clicked her tongue and shuddered. "Why you?" She sobbed, falling against his chest as his arms came around her. "What if you're gone for another year?"

Rhett's hands rubbed her back. "I understand if you don't want to wait for me." He sounded husky and as broken as she felt.

Mia pulled away from him. "Of course I'm going to wait for you, Rhett! Stop being stupid. But what about the wedding?"

Rhett chuckled, but his expression sobered again. "We'll have to postpone it until the deployment ends. I'm so sorry."

Mia pressed her lips together and said nothing. What could she say?

Rhett caressed her cheeks. "We only have tonight, and it's already late."

Mia shook her head and brushed her lips against his. "I don't *care!* We only have *tonight,* Rhett, like you just said. I'm tired of waiting. I don't wanna waste it."

Rhett held her gaze in his, so steady and soft and warm. "Are you sure?"

Mia clung to him like her life depended on it. "I'm sure. If it's what you want—no more waiting."

Rhett leaned forward. "No more waiting," he whispered. This time, when he kissed her, it consumed her world.

For just that single, blissful night, nothing else mattered but them.

3

Saying goodbye to Rhett again had been the hardest thing she'd ever done, even harder than last time. Why, Mia had no idea. Perhaps it had been the thought of him finally coming home, the wedding, the thought that they'd finally get a chance to start their life together only to have that opportunity ripped away from them both.

She did nothing the rest of the day the morning he left. Maybe it was pathetic of her, but she sat curled up on the couch with a blanket, alternating between crying and just staring into space or trying to imagine Rhett with his other Navy SEAL buddies and them getting on a plane and heading to only God-knew-where.

Mia's phone rang. She blinked slowly, peering at the night sky outside the window. She rubbed her thick eyes and peeked at her phone. To her surprise, she had several missed calls—one from her father, three from her mother along with a few text messages, a text from a friend with another possible gig, and Rhett's mom.

Mia dialed her number back.

"Mia?" Donna's voice cracked.

"Yeah, sorry I missed your call." Mia cleared her throat, trying not to cry.

"I wanted to make sure you were okay after Rhett left this morning." Donna's voice sounded thick with tears.

Mia's heart tightened like someone had squeezed it. "It's been hard. How are you and Edward holding up?"

Donna released a shaky breath. "We've been doing a lot of praying. We're planning to go to the church tomorrow to help with the picnic. Why don't you come with us or meet us there? I think it would be a good distraction we all need right now."

Mia bit her lower lip. The thought of another lonely day in this apartment with only memories of Rhett to keep her company felt unbearable. "Y–yeah, sure. That sounds good."

Maybe keeping herself busy would help. But as she and Donna finished up the conversation and hung up, leaving Mia alone in her apartment, she realized one horrible thing.

Nothing would help her accept the fact that her fiancé had once again been deployed out to a war zone to fight for his life—nothing.

•••

Mia tried to keep herself distracted in the first month after Rhett left again. It wasn't easy, especially when she didn't hear from him beyond a text saying, *I love you. I won't be able to contact you for a few months. Be safe.* It left her with too many questions and not enough answers. Where was he being sent? Would he come home after those few months ended? How many months were a few? Had his deployment been extended? Why wouldn't he have a phone or be able to contact her? Was it only her he couldn't contact or his parents too?

Dinner with her father, Travis, one weekend went as well as could be expected. The food, made by the cook Travis always hired, tasted delicious. It made sitting through her father's lecture bearable. Travis droned on about the direction her life was going, how she needed to "get a real job" and find a more "stable" husband to provide for her. She tried to see it from her dad's perspective. Maybe in some twisted way he was genuinely trying to protect her from what he saw as a job that wouldn't provide for her, a husband who would be gone for months or years at a time, and a life that wouldn't be good for her. It still angered her, but she said nothing, not wanting to fight with him or cause unnecessary drama. She'd always been one to shy away from conflict, the kind of person to try to avoid it at any costs, even if it meant she clammed up and didn't voice her thoughts or opinions. She expected it probably came from some sort of trauma associated with watching her parents fight all the time as a kid until their divorce, but therapy was expensive, and honestly, church worked better anyway.

Life continued on.

Mia held her guitar in her hands with a piece of paper on the table in front of her the day after Christmas. She strummed notes to the scribbled lyrics that had played in her mind as she woke that morning. Her hands shifted between the chords as she hummed the tune, bouncing her head to it.

A knock thudded on the door.

"Uh, just a minute!" Mia called. She grinned, leaning her guitar against the table carefully to make sure it didn't fall, and then set her mom's binder of recipes on top of the paper with the music. She usually preferred no one read or see her songs until she completed them. Clearing her throat, she rushed over to the door and opened it. "Can I help ...?" Her voice trailed off at the sight before her.

A man stood in a Navy uniform, and she shook her head as her body trembled. He would only be here for one reason, and she couldn't face that reason, didn't want to—couldn't.

"N–no ..." Mia held her hands over her mouth as her knees wobbled.

"Are you Mia Yarding?"

Mia nodded, unable to speak. *God please,* she mentally prayed. *Please let him be alive. Don't let this be—*

"I'm so sorry to have to tell you this, Mia, but Rhett Callum has gone MIA while on his latest mission." His gaze softened on her.

"MIA ... wh–what does that mean?" Mia's eyes widened.

"It means he's gone missing in action, ma'am."

Mia shook her head, not sure how to feel, how to process it. "I don't ... um, I mean, is anyone looking for him?"

The man pressed his lips together in a firm line. "They looked for a while and had an investigation open, but recently, new evidence has come to light, and he's been presumed dead. I am so sorry."

"Presumed dead?" Mia blinked. "I don't ... I don't understand. Wh–what do you mean presumed dead? H–how do you know? Wh ...?"

The man frowned. "It means that the investigation was closed, and he's considered missing in action, presumed dead. Once again, I am so sorry, ma'am. Is there anything I can do for you?"

Mia blinked at him, staggering backward as she turned and leaned against the door frame. Her legs collapsed, and she sat in the doorway as the tears finally spilled over. Her stomach lurched, and she felt as if she was going to be sick. "He's ... he's dead? Y–you're sure? What if ... what if he's still out there?"

The man shook his head as he crouched beside her. "Based on the evidence, which has been classified due to the nature of the mission he was on, it's likely he's ... he's dead, ma'am."

"Likely?" She snapped the word and glared at him even though she realized this man didn't deserve her anger.

The man nodded. "Yes, ma'am. They wouldn't have classified him as presumed dead without evidence to suggest it. I am sorry and wish I could tell you more."

What could she say? *Thank you for telling me my fiancé is dead?*

"Can I get you anything? Do you have someone who can come sit with you?" he asked.

Mia nodded, but she didn't look at him, couldn't process anything but the fact that *Rhett was gone.*

No. She couldn't believe it, didn't believe it. Her mind raced until it hit a sliver of hope. Mia grabbed the door frame and used it to help herself stand. She only managed a curt nod to the soldier before she closed her door and rushed inside to get her phone.

Rhett's Navy SEAL buddies loved each other like brothers, closer than brothers, after everything they had gone through together.

What had the number been?

Rhett held out the phone to her. "Look, if anything happens to me, or I'm gone and you need help, or need to find out more about me, call this number. It'll get you in contact with Blake Hastings—he's a good man, and no matter what, he'll be able to help. Okay?"

Mia closed her eyes, trying to picture the number he had typed into her phone. He hadn't wanted her to save it, but she'd always been a visual learner, so seeing it typed out on her phone had helped her memorize it—at the time.

The numbers came back to her, so she typed them in, sucked in a deep breath, and dialed Blake's number.

"Hello?" The voice on the other end sounded exhausted and worn—and most definitely female.

"Um, hi. I'm looking for Blake Hastings." Her heart pounded furiously in her chest, and her stomach clenched.

"He's ... um, he's unavailable right now." The voice hitched, cracking to the point of tears.

God, please no, Mia silently prayed. Horror washed over her, and she sat down on the couch before she collapsed again. "Um ..." Mia choked. "I'm ... I'm Mia Yarding, Rhett Callum's fiancé. I just ... um, I heard—heard that he–that he ..." She couldn't get the words out, couldn't speak, couldn't even *breathe* behind the lump in her throat. "That he ..."

The voice murmured softly, but Mia couldn't make the words out. "Um, just a moment. I'm with one of the Navy SEALs on Rhett and Blake's team. Um, here."

"This is Jake." The new soft male voice had a bit of a Southern twang to it. "You're Rhett's fiancé?"

"Y–yes." Mia nodded even though he couldn't see her.

Jake grunted, a low, deep sound. "He spoke 'bout you a lot. Listen, uh, Blake's been hurt pretty bad. I'm here with his girlfriend, Lillian, y'know, the one who answered his phone. Did you call 'bout Rhett?"

"Y–yes. A soldier just came by and told me ... told me that ..." The lump in her throat grew. Her chest *ached.* "Um, that he's MIA. Presumed dead."

Jake stayed silent for an agonizing minute that made her wonder whether he had hung up on her. "Yeah." He muttered a curse. "Um, listen, the mission we were on, it's been classified. I can't talk 'bout it. But they investigated, looked for a body, didn't find one. It was ... He wasn't the only SEAL who's gone MIA, and we have two more who got injured, near death right now. I wish I could help you, but that's all I can say."

Mia covered her mouth with her free hand and sobbed into it. "Is he really ... is Rhett really ...?" She couldn't say it.

Jake slowly exhaled. It sounded exhausted, worn, pained. "What happened out there ... yeah. Yeah, he's dead, Mia. I'm—" He choked and cleared his throat, but it ended in another curse.

Mia nearly dropped the phone. She trembled, shivering as if she stood in zero-degree weather, unable to stop shaking. "Oh, God. Oh, God. Oh, God, *please* ..." She panted, unable to breathe, unable to say anything else as she rocked on the couch, trembling and sobbing. The sobs turned into wails.

Rhett wouldn't be coming back. Rhett, the man she loved, was dead.

4

Mia completely shut down. Every day that passed after hearing the news about Rhett became more difficult for her to wake up, to take a shower, to eat, to do anything. No more song lyrics or tunes played in her head. Mia didn't touch her guitar. She only texted her mom and family members briefly to let them know she was okay. Eventually, her mother stopped believing it and came over. She forced Mia to get up, get dressed, and made her a meal that she didn't feel like eating.

A week after the news about Rhett, his mom called to let Mia know they were having a small ceremony for him. "We–we waited for news ... hoping ... hoping something would change, but ..." Donna's voice broke, and she sniffed. "Will you come?"

"Of course," Mia whispered.

Out of respect, she decided to text Blake's number and let them all know. *Hi, it's Mia, Rhett's fiancé. I've been praying for Blake and the other SEALs Jake said were injured; I hope they pull through. Will you please let Jake and the others know that Rhett's family is having a ceremony for him? Just in case they wanted to know. They're always welcome.* She called Donna to make sure it was okay, and Donna thanked her since she had no way to get ahold of any of the SEALs on Rhett's team. Mia texted Blake's number with the time and date.

Mia's mom stayed with her, and the day of the ceremony, she wore a simple black dress—the one she always wore to funerals.

"Are you ready?" Mia's mother asked. Elaine's kind, round face softened as she straightened out the simple black dress she wore. Her mom kept her hair cut short, and it had grayed out years ago. But something about the aged wrinkles lining her mother's face comforted her, reminding her that she wasn't alone in this.

Mia rubbed at her burning eyes. "To say goodbye to the man I loved? When we don't even have a body? Never." She shook her head and fell into her mother's arms. "No, I'll never be ready for that, Mama."

Elaine held her for the longest time. Each step to the car made Mia's legs feel like they weighed a thousand pounds. They stayed silent on the way to the cemetery, and Mia said another prayer for Blake and other SEALs on Rhett's team, asking God to help them make it through.

Rhett's parents, Donna and Edward, already stood at the cemetery when Mia and Elaine arrived. They all four exchanged hugs, and she greeted Rhett's maternal grandparents, his aunt and uncle, and his cousins. The pastor arrived, along with some other people in town who knew Rhett and his family. The pastor began speaking about Rhett and his life, the kind of man he was, and how hard he worked in this town and in life.

Mia tried to hold back the tears, but they fell down her cheeks in waves as he spoke. Beside her, Donna handed her a tissue and squeezed her hand in comfort.

Out of the corner of her eye, she spotted two men at the edge of the crowd. Both wore Navy uniforms and saluted when the other soldiers shot off their guns. The pastor finished reading a Bible verse and led them all in prayer.

The soldiers folded up a flag and handed it to Donna and Edward. Both of them cried, and Edward hung his head and pinched his nose while Donna clutched the flag tightly against her chest.

They had no body to bury and no casket, but Donna and Edward had paid for a headstone and a place on site. Watching Donna clutch the flag, seeing and hearing the guns go off as they honored Rhett ... it became too much for Mia. She darted away from the site to the edge of the crowd. Resting a hand against the trunk of a tree, she took shallow breaths and doubled over. For a moment, she thought she would vomit, and her stomach twisted with nausea. It had become normal these last few weeks—to feel sick at all hours of the day, to get dizzy whenever she stood, her appetite had vanished, and she felt tired and utterly exhausted. But given her grief, it made sense. The grief had even caused her to skip her period, but she often had irregular periods, so skipping one, especially when stressed, wasn't unusual.

Wiping her eyes with a tissue, Mia straightened and struggled not to vomit.

The two men in Navy uniforms walked down the road, heading to a vehicle parked at the edge of the cemetery. "Wait!" Mia called, sprinting up to them. "Did–did you know Rhett?" She blinked tears out of her eyes.

The one on the right nodded, while the one on the left—shorter and stockier but still far taller and stronger than her—answered first. "Yes, ma'am."

The one on the right had a scraggly beard. "Are you Mia?" His smooth country twang sounded familiar.

Mia nodded. "Yeah. Jake?"

Jake rubbed his scraggly beard with another nod. "Yes, ma'am. This is Nate. We were both on the same team as Rhett. Malcolm and Blake would've been here too, but they're still in bad shape."

Mia swallowed and wrapped her arms around her stomach that still welled with nausea. "I've been praying for them. Thank you for being here f–for Rhett." Her voice broke, and she blinked out more tears.

Nate glared at the ground, shoving his hands into his pockets, while Jake held out his hand. "It's the least we could do for 'im after everything he's done for us."

After an awkward goodbye, Mia headed off and slipped in her mom's car. She leaned back against the passenger seat.

"Why don't you come back to my place?" Elaine turned the car on and kept it in neutral as they waited for other cars behind them to leave. "It'll be good for both of us, I think. Plus, I could take care of you. I don't like having such an empty nest. I could have Elizabeth over."

Elizabeth, or Beth, as Mia had grown up calling her, had been her godmother. Mia had never known her mother's parents, and her father's parents died before she'd been born, so the only sort of grandparent she had ever known was Beth.

"Maybe later this week. I think I just wanna go home and sleep for a while." Mia closed her eyes. They felt so tired and heavy, and she felt so sick of crying. Crying wouldn't bring Rhett back. "I think I'm coming down with the flu."

Elaine exhaled. "All the more reason for me to take care of you, honey."

"Mom, I'll be fine. I just need ... time." Mia rubbed her face without opening her eyes. "Time to rest and process all of this. And to pray." She added that last part mostly to reassure her mother. If she was being honest, her heart didn't feel like praying.

God could have kept Rhett safe. Could have brought him home. But He didn't. Mia didn't want to think those thoughts, but they festered in her mind anyway. But for now, she just needed to go home and sleep.

At least in sleep, she could have some sort of peace.

5

After vomiting for the millionth time, Mia slumped over to the bathroom sink. She had tried to turn on the water to brush her teeth and take a much-needed shower, but the water wouldn't turn on. Not to mention the overwhelmingly strong minty scent of the toothpaste sent her stomach reeling again.

She wiped at her swollen, heavy eyes as if she could wipe away the grief. Another month had come and gone, one where she had only gotten a few gigs, just enough to make the rent. Her utilities and water must have been shut off, and Mia ...

She couldn't bring herself to care. What did it matter whether she had electricity and water? What did any of it matter? Rhett was dead, and his death had destroyed any hope Mia'd had for any sort of future. Her hopes and dreams—of a life with Rhett, of a family—they had died with him.

Electricity meant nothing. Water meant nothing. Food meant nothing. Life ... It all meant nothing without Rhett. Mia slammed a hand against the handle of the sink a little too hard and grimaced from the pain radiating through her hand. She tilted her head back and *laughed,* but it sounded empty, crazed.

No, without Rhett ... facing another day, another hour without him, knowing he would never come back, seemed unbearable. It felt impossible.

As another wave of nausea hit her, Mia slumped onto the couch and tried her best to forget, to sleep it all away.

•••

Mia still hadn't started her period. At first, she just suspected she skipped it because of all the stress of losing Rhett. But she couldn't possibly have had the flu for the last month.

She couldn't even think of the possibility, the idea that she could be ...

No, it couldn't — *wouldn't* — be. Yet she went to the store and bought a test anyway—multiple tests, just to be sure.

She took them all and waited—waited for three minutes to decide her future, the future that now lay in front of her, darker than ever.

The first one came back positive. So did the second, and so did the third. By the fourth, Mia realized the truth, one she didn't want to face, no—one she didn't know *how* to face.

She was pregnant.

•••

Going to the doctor would make it real. And other than her one free health care check-up once a year, she hadn't been to the doctor in ages. Who had the money for that, anyway? She certainly didn't. No, it would only add an extra bill she couldn't afford to pay, and the tests had basically confirmed what she didn't want to be true.

Mia parked her car in the driveway of the house Rhett had been building. She stepped out and stared at the wooden boards and tools Rhett had left out before being deployed. Tears fell from her eyes as she walked the ground, gazing at the ghosts of what might have been.

Once, she had wanted nothing more than a family with Rhett. Even if they had a child as soon as they married, she wouldn't have minded. He, being an only child, had always wanted a sibling, and Mia had always wished she had been closer with her sister. Mia and Rhett had spoken for hours about their dreams for the future, including raising a big family. Finances had concerned Mia ever since her father had cut her off, but Rhett had reassured her that he would take care of them. They both wanted time to just be married, of course, but if God had chosen to bless them with a little miracle, then Mia would have been happy.

Would have been.

That dream had died along with Rhett and whatever horrors he had faced, horrors that Mia hadn't even been told because it had been classified, horrors that had prevented them from even having a body to bury. At night, she dreamed about it—about gunfights in a desert, places she didn't know or understand. Sometimes, she would see Rhett here or even back at her house, reaching out for her and groaning in pain.

Mia's stomach clenched with nausea. For a moment, she plopped down in the grass outside the skeleton of a house and breathed through her nose to try to avoid vomiting. When it passed, she felt shaky and realized she hadn't eaten yet today.

What would her future look like without him but with this ... this ...? Mia held a hand over her stomach with a frown. What business did she have trying to raise a child? On her own? She'd be a single mother, unable to put food on the table or even keep the electricity on. Her dreams of being a singer would shatter. She'd likely have to stay home, but if she did that, how would she find work?

The menial jobs around here, even if she did manage to find one, wouldn't be enough to pay for rent, food, electricity, and countless other bills much less all the expenses of having and raising a child. Who would provide for her while she cared for an infant and recovered after having it? What ...

What if something happened medically?

All the possibilities flashed into her mind, endless problems without solutions. But every single one of them ended up at the sole, agonizing reason why she couldn't have this child.

Because Rhett wasn't here with her.

6

Perhaps Mia went to talk to her father because she knew he'd confirm what she already suspected, what she had already thought about. Maybe deep down inside, she wanted this baby, but without Rhett, she didn't want *anything.* Not a house, not her singing career, not her music, and certainly not a walking, breathing reminder of what she had lost.

Mia's father, Travis, sat behind the desk in his office, typing away at his computer as he talked on the phone. He wore his typical suit and tie, looking professional as usual. For his age, he still had a full head of black hair that matched hers, now lined with silver, and a pot belly but a perfectly smooth, clean-shaven face. He eyed her with a frown when she walked in but quickly returned to his work. Mia sat down in the chair across from him as if she was one of his clients. Years of hard work had left him owning the major radio station, newspaper, and TV station in town, and he worked from his office many times. Eventually, he had expanded to own and control most of the media around town.

Travis hung up the phone and peered at her around his computer with a frown. "You look horrible, Mia. Please tell me you've been doing more than moping around the house. It isn't good for you."

Mia flinched. "I just lost the man I loved and planned to spend the rest of my life with. What else do you expect me to do?"

Travis sighed, shoving the top of his laptop down. "Honey, I expect you to move on. We will all die eventually, and, yes, losing someone before their time is difficult. I'm only telling you this because I love you. But I did warn you—planning a life with a man in the military would have only ended in heartbreak, one way or another. This was exactly what I was afraid of when you first got involved with him—"

"I'm pregnant," she blurted, interrupting him.

Travis blinked, and his mouth opened as if he didn't register what she'd said.

"I'm pregnant." Mia repeated the words, unsure whether she fully even registered them herself. It still didn't seem real—couldn't be real.

Travis pinched the bridge of his nose with a deep, sharp inhale. "Pregnant?" He spat the word like a curse. "Pregnant with his child?"

Mia nodded, frowning. "I haven't been with anyone else ..."

"You shouldn't have been sleeping with him before you married him, Mia!" Travis muttered a curse. "What ... what exactly are you going to do? You don't have a real job, not one that could provide for a child. My God, Mia, do you even understand the gravity of what this means, the responsibility it will take for you to raise a child, especially one on your own? How are you supposed to be a mother?"

Mia flinched at every word that cut her like a knife. She wanted to say so much to him. *How would you? You abandoned Mom and I, left her alone to raise me by herself. What would you know about parental responsibility?* But she clamped her mouth shut. When he finished, she said, "I know. I can't–I can't have this baby."

Travis furrowed his eyebrows. "You could terminate it."

Mia froze, staring at him. She had already thought about the possibility of that, but hearing it out loud ... It made her feel weird. Her stomach churned, but she chalked that up to the morning sickness—or day sickness, since it seemed to happen all day and not just in the morning. "I had already thought of that, but I wasn't ... I wasn't sure about the cost."

She wouldn't ask him, not directly.

Travis sighed, staring out the window. "I'll pay for it. This will all just ... go away." He stood, shoving his hands into his pockets as he stood in front of the window open to their large backyard. "I'll give you the money. You can make an appointment, and then maybe you can finally see that this lifestyle you've chosen to live isn't good for you. I want what's best for you, Mia." Travis finally turned and met her eyes with brown ones that matched hers. "Come back and work for me again. You'll do much better off, and you'll finally be able to get you a nice place."

Mia pursed her lips. "One step at a time."

Travis nodded, fishing for his wallet. He handed her a wad of cash. "Use it only for this termination. If you need anything else, give me a call."

Give me a call. Like she was one of his clients.

Mia nodded and stood from the chair. She didn't feel anything, just ... numb. She felt so numb, in fact, that she didn't even realize she had walked to her car until she sat in the driver's seat.

Go see your mother. Where the thought had come from, she had no idea. But she ignored it. No, she needed to get this done and over with, starting with making an appointment. Her mother would have to wait until later.

Mia left the radio off as she drove to the abortion clinic in town. Normally, she would have listened to music, singing or humming along, but this time, she didn't. She stayed silent as she pulled into the parking lot and stared at the building.

God ... But she had no words, no prayer. What could she say? She couldn't pray, couldn't invite Him into ... into all this. "If You wanted me to have a baby, You wouldn't have let Rhett get killed!" she screamed, sobbing as she gripped the steering wheel until her knuckles ached. She pounded her hands on it again and again, screaming unintelligible words to unleash all the grief and pain and anger that she held inside.

Her father's words echoed in her mind. *"My God, Mia, do you even understand the gravity of what this means, the responsibility it will take for you to raise a child, especially one on your own? How are you supposed to be a mother?"*

Mia wiped furiously at her eyes, grabbed her purse, and headed out of her car and into the abortion clinic.

7

For the dozenth time, Mia read over the information that the clinic had given her. They had charged her for a urine test to see how far along she was and got back to her with the results in a few days. According to it, she was ten weeks along, which meant she would come in tomorrow to take the first set of pills and then take the second set two days later at home when she would "pass the pregnancy."

You will never be a mother—not a good one, Mia thought to herself. She paced in her living room, mentally listing out all the reasons why she couldn't bring a child into the world—not into this.

Mia stubbed her toe on the TV tray as she walked by. She cursed, grabbing it as the pain hit and stole her breath. As she doubled over, a wave of dizziness hit, so she fell to the ground with a quiet cry. At night, with her electricity shut off, she couldn't see and had been stumbling around in the dark. "I can't ... I can't do this. I can't bring a child into this!" she sobbed.

Your mother will help you. When the thought hit, Mia shook her head, shouting into the dark as if the thought had been spoken to her out loud by a real person.

Yes, her mother would probably help her, but she couldn't do this. Without Rhett, she wouldn't be a good mother. She couldn't just live with her mom. How could she? When her mom already struggled enough as it was? When her mom had raised her and her sister alone as a single mother? When they had scrapped their whole lives because her father had never been there? She couldn't do that to her mom, especially in her older age. With her aging and bad health, her mom wouldn't be able to raise a child and take care of Mia financially, not when her mom basically lived on disability.

No, terminating this pregnancy would be best for everyone. Mia refused to be a burden to the mother who had sacrificed her whole life for her and her sister. Her mom had given up all her dreams to provide for them, working double shifts and struggling to keep things afloat. She refused to be a burden on her mom any longer. And this? Her father had already paid for it. It would be ... it would be easy.

So why did she feel so heavy? So ... sick and heartbroken?

It's because of Rhett. You're still grieving for Rhett. That's all. This ... this is a good thing. It's a good thing, Mia told herself.

A knock thudded at her door.

"Mia? Mia, it's your mother. I've been calling and texting you, and I'm worried about you."

No, her mother couldn't see her like this, couldn't find out. Mia rushed to stand up in her panic, but a wave of dizziness threw her back down.

"Mia, what was that? I'm coming in." Elaine opened the door Mia must have forgotten to lock and marched in. She frowned. "Mia, I can't see a thing, what—" She shined her phone light into the living room, and the beam landed on Mia on the floor. "Mia, what's wrong? Why are you on the floor, and why are all the lights off?" Elaine hobbled over to her and bent down to help Mia up. When she did, Elaine guided her onto the couch. "Are you still sick? You've been struggling for the last month. I think we should take you to the doctor." She pursed her lips and gazed at the dark house. "Honey, are your ... Have your utilities been turned off?"

Mia's cheeks heated as she swallowed back bile and leaned her head back against the couch. "I ... Yes, okay! I'm a failure! My electricity's been shut off, and I'm—I know I'm a failure!" She hadn't meant to snap at her mom and honestly had no idea where the anger and frustration came from.

If it bothered Elaine, she didn't show it. Her eyes only softened in the phone light shining between them. "Mia, talk to me. Please tell me what's going on."

Mia shook her head. "I can't, Mom! I can't because if I do, then you'll ... then you'll ..." She couldn't get the words out.

"Then I'll what?" Elaine shot her the "Mom" expression.

Mia reached out to clutch her mom, and Elaine wrapped her arms around her. For a long time, Mia felt safe, like she was home, like the rest of her problems ceased to exist. But then reality hit, and the moment ended. She pulled away. "Please, Mom, just ... just don't worry about it. I'm still just ... grieving over Rhett." Her voice broke, and fresh tears exploded out of her eyes. She sighed, wiping at them, but then thought, *What's the use?* Mia didn't really stop crying at all these days.

"I'm your mother. I can sense that there's something more going on. Honestly, the Holy Spirit made me feel like I needed to come here tonight ... told me that you *needed* me." Elaine grabbed Mia's hands and gently held them. "Please tell me what's really wrong. Whatever it is, I am here. I will always be here."

Mia pulled away from her and wrapped her knees up to her chest. She rested her arms on her knees and stuck her head on top of them as if she could hide and make herself smaller. "I'm pregnant," she murmured. It still didn't feel real.

Elaine's eyes widened but then softened on her. "Oh, honey ..."

Mia swallowed, and another wave of nausea welled up in her. "I'm pregnant, and I made an appointment tomorrow to terminate it."

Elaine flinched. She blinked several times and then reached out to draw Mia against her chest. "Honey ..." The word sounded soft, warm, pained, but not ... not judgmental, not hateful or disgusted or angry like Mia had been expecting. When they pulled away, Mia wiped at her eyes again, and Elaine handed her a tissue. "What makes you feel like that's your only option?"

Mia laughed, but it sounded empty and broken. "Look around, Mom! I–I can't even take care of myself much less a kid! Rhett and I wanted kids in the future, but I can't bring a child into this. I can't–I can't do this." She shook her head, running her fingers through her long, thick hair. "Dad gave me the money."

Elaine frowned. "Travis knows? And he gave you the money to do this?" Her voice dripped with anger, barely contained.

Mia looked away but nodded.

"Honey, believe me when I tell you that no matter what circumstances you're in, killing the child is never the right thing."

Biting her lip, Mia glared at her mother even though logically she knew her mom didn't deserve any of her rage. Mia often dumped out her true feelings to her mom, who never deserved it. But Elaine always loved her anyway.

"I know you managed to raise us, Mom, but this is different."

Elaine shook her head. "No, honey, it isn't. Listen to me. There's something I've never told you."

Mia rested her head on her knees again, not bothering to wipe away the tears. "What?"

"Around the time I got pregnant with you, Travis left shortly after that, and when I told him I was pregnant, he wanted nothing to do with the baby—you." Elaine blinked, and tears fell from her eyes. Her expression looked so pained, so guilty, that it made Mia's stomach twist, but she stayed silent to let her mom talk. "I had no money, no job. Your father's reputation around town kept a lot of people from hiring me. He made it seem like I left him when I didn't. I had no family support, so ..." Elaine shook her head and held a hand over her mouth. "I made an appointment. It wasn't as easy back then, but I did it. I even walked up to the clinic doors on the day my appointment had been made—to kill you."

The words hit her like a physical blow. Mia flinched, unfurling and turning to fully face her mom. Her heart tightened, and she felt like she couldn't breathe. "Y–you almost aborted me?"

Elaine nodded, and she sobbed as she turned and grabbed Mia's hands in her own. "Yes, I did, and it's been my biggest regret in life."

Mia clutched her mom's hands, blinking at the tears that blurred her vision. "Wh–what stopped you?"

Elaine smiled through the tears. "Your godmother—Elizabeth. She ... she was walking on the sidewalk and saw me hesitate in front of the door. She asked me if I was thinking about getting an abortion, and I said yes, afraid she would judge me, but instead she only said, 'Before you do, will you please do me a small favor?' When I asked her what, she simply said, 'My husband I were never able to have any children of our own. It's a blessing to bring life into this world. So, before you make a decision you can't take back, will you think about it first?' And I did. I told her my story, and we stayed in contact. She helped me with everything—took me to all my appointments, helped me financially, and she's the reason why you're alive today, Mia. She's the reason why I didn't abort you."

Mia fell onto her mother, sobbing so hard she couldn't breathe. The whole time, her mom held her, rubbing her back and clutching her like she became a safety net that Mia needed.

"Elizabeth and I will help you. No matter what anyone else tells you, no matter what you think about yourself or your circumstances, you will make a great mother, Mia. Because God wouldn't have given you this blessing, this little miracle, if you weren't meant to be one, if He didn't have a plan already in place for you and your baby—Rhett's baby. I know you had a life planned and dreams planned with him. And I know you're grieving and that you miss him."

At that, Mia choked out another sob.

"But, honey, this child is a piece of him, a piece of him that God gave you as a gift—one to hold and cherish, one to remember Rhett. And whatever difficulties you face, Elizabeth will be here, I will be here, and God will be here too. Let Him be your guide—your safety, your provider, your protector. God is everything you need, and He will see you through this."

Mia nodded, peering out the window at the night sky above. The stars twinkled overhead, bright and beautiful, reminding her that God knew each one by name. If He created the stars, knew each one by name, He had formed this baby. He knew the baby, knew his or her name, knew the future laid out before her. Maybe Mia needed to start trusting God instead of looking at the circumstances around her.

Whatever happened, whatever the future held, God would see her through, and this life .... This precious life inside her deserved to be saved.

EPILOGUE

Rhett and another SEAL on his team, Leon, stumbled through the mountainous terrain, covered in blood and gaping wounds. Rhett shoved it all aside, thinking of Mia. He had to get back to her.

"Just ... just over this next hill. There's a town," Rhett rasped as he half-dragged, half carried Leon's body forward. He put the pain in a box where it didn't touch him. *God, get us home,* he prayed. It had been his prayer, the mantra he'd clung to when the terrorists they had attacked on their mission had found them and captured him and Leon. It had kept them both alive so far. "Once in the town ..." Rhett winced, coughing again as he stumbled over a branch and staggered down the sharp incline. "We'll get to our allies. Find a base. Get home."

Leon's eyes glazed over. "I don't ... I'm not gonna make it. We're not gonna make it."

Rhett gripped him tighter and trudged forward. Branches snagged on his ripped uniform, and he wished he had a rifle in his hands. His left still had a chain on it from when he and Leon had managed to escape. It caught on a branch, and his ankle twisted on a rock as he tried to make his way down the hill. "We'll make it," he rasped. "We'll get back home to our families."

Yes, he would make it back home to Mia ... to their life they both wanted to start together.

No matter what else happened, somehow, Rhett would find his way back home to her.

•••

"There." Mia grinned as she, Elaine, Elizabeth, and Donna finally finished setting up the crib and rocking chair beside her bed in her apartment. "It's a work in progress, but I like it." And she did. As Mia gazed at her room that they half converted into a nursery, she felt ... happy—joyful for the first time since Rhett's death.

In a week, she would sing at Nate and his fiancé Denee's wedding. The money would help her with her bills piling up. Donna, when Elaine and Mia had told her, wanted to help and be involved in the baby's life too. "That little miracle is the last piece of my son," Donna had said.

The three women had become a lifeline. Not a day went by that Mia didn't thank God for her mother, godmother, and mother-in-law. Even though Rhett had died, Mia still saw Donna as a mother too.

She would be one soon. It still terrified her, the thought of failing. The future loomed ahead of her, but Mia felt ready. God would see her through, somehow, and He had planned this for a reason. He saw her as a mother, had chosen this time to give her a child even though she didn't understand it. Some days, she still got angry. Others, she could barely get out of bed in her grief. But with prayer and reliance on God, she could do this—raise a child, be a mother to the life God wanted her to save, the mother God called her to be.

A knock thudded on the door.

"Are you expecting company?" Elaine asked.

Mia shook her head. "No. I'll go see who it is." Mia left the nursery behind and went to open the door.

When she did ... Mia couldn't believe her eyes. No. Surely it had to be a mistake or her mind hallucinating what she wanted to see.

"Mia." The choked word came from the man standing in the doorway in front of her. It sounded relieved, pained, and broken.

"Rhett?" Mia gasped, struggling to breathe, to believe what she saw as she took in the sight of him before her. His tanned skin had become pale, he'd lost weight and had scars, both fresh and new, littering his skin. Bandages covered him, and baggy clothes too big for him now that he'd lost weight hung loosely off him. "Is it ... is it really you?" She couldn't—

Rhett nodded and reached out for her. Tears fell from his blue, bloodshot eyes. "I'm home. I'm home, Mia."

"You're alive." Mia couldn't believe it. Shock rippled through her. "I thought you were dead." The word broke her. She threw herself at him. His arms came around her as he buried his face in her neck, but the choked sobs coming from him made her heart twist. "You're really alive?" It sounded like a half question and half declaration. Mia couldn't stop grasping him, keeping his arms around his chest and onto his back.

Rhett winced but didn't let her go as they pulled back just enough to stare at each other. Tears streaked down his cheeks. "Yeah, I'm–I'm alive. God got us through."

"Rhett? Son." Donna sobbed, and she and Rhett collapsed against one another. Everyone in the room sobbed and cried, and Mia couldn't let go of his arm even as he clung to his mom.

"What happened to you?" Mia asked. "They told us you were M.I.A., presumed dead. Even your Navy SEAL buddies thought you were." Mia stared and stared at him, clinging to him with all her strength as if he would disappear if she let him go.

He turned from his mom to embrace her again as he swallowed. "I'm home now. That's all that matters." His eyes flicked down to her baby bump. "Mia, you're ...?"

Mia smiled, choking out a laugh through her relieved, joyful tears. "I'm pregnant. We're going to have a baby. You're ... you're going to be a father."

Rhett collapsed into her and she into him as they cried together. She didn't want to let him go, not even as Donna called his father to tell him of the miracle.

God, Mia thought in a prayer. *I am so sorry I didn't trust You.* God had given her two miracles—her baby, and now Rhett ... here, *alive,* with her again. He had lived. Mia would have to tell him the news, what she had almost done in her grief, but she would tell him of how God had used her mother and the history there to convince Mia to save this precious life inside her.

And now, despite whatever horrors Rhett had gone through, they could finally start their life together, their family, after all. And whatever they had to face, God would get them through.

Joanna White is a Christian Author and fangirl. *Hunter* and *Shifter* are the first two books in her debut series, called the Valiant Series. She writes Fantasy, Science Fiction, Contemporary Romance, Historical Fiction, Nonfiction, and more. Her short stories have been featured in several anthologies.

She graduated from Full Sail University with a BFA in Creative Writing For Entertainment. Ever since she was ten years old, she's been writing stories and has a deep passion for writing and creating stories, worlds, characters, and plots that readers can immerse themselves in. In 2020, she reached her personal goal of writing a million words in a year. Most of all, Joanna loves God, her family, staying at home, and being a total nerd.

To stay updated and find out more about her novels, where her inspiration comes from, games, giveaways, and more, visit her website at **https://authorjoannawhite.com**

1:30 P.M.

BY ALLEN STEADHAM

"For thou hast possessed my reins: thou hast covered me in my mother's womb. I will praise thee; for I am fearfully and wonderfully made: marvellous are thy works; and that my soul knoweth right well. My substance was not hid from thee, when I was made in secret, and curiously wrought in the lowest parts of the earth. Thine eyes did see my substance, yet being unperfect; and in thy book all my members were written, which in continuance were fashioned, when as yet there was none of them."

– Psalms 139: 13-16 (King James Version)

3:32 P.M. SATURDAY MAY 11TH - LOGGIEWORLD AMUSEMENT PARK – CHESTERFIELD, MISSOURI

"C'mon, Julie! Let's do this!" my boyfriend says enthusiastically as he pulls on my right arm. I giggle and start running ahead, now dragging Chet towards the "World in Motion" roller coaster line. I look back to see his shaggy, wheat-colored hair flowing in the wind. "You are seriously messing with me!" he says with a laugh as he runs to catch up with me. "You said you were scared of that stuff!" Beyond the ride lies a gorgeous blue May sky with just a few clouds. I'm laughing too much to answer him. A few seconds later, we stop at the back of the line.

"I am, but this is *our* trip," I reply.

He grins and leans to the side, clapping his hands together. "Alright, let's go!"

This roller-coaster is intimidating. The big sign above us reads "World in Motion: The world's second tallest roller coaster." Gazing up and to my left, I see the current riders ascending slowly. With a near-instant drop, they scream in excitement and terror as they wind down to the bottom before being scooped up once more. I thought I felt my stomach drop when they did, but I won't back out now.

Chet's been watching, too, his feet bouncing up and down. "Look at them over there screamin' like that!" he says.

Six minutes later, we're shouting our joy to the skies, though Chet looks like he might puke. He's grinning like a goof as we reach one of the peaks but shuts his eyes and turns his head away as we shoot down into rapid spiraling. "Closing your eyes makes it worse!" I yell over the sounds of the roller coaster and the other riders. I laugh at his expense because he's the one who insisted we get on this monster.

Once we're off, he tries to act cool again. "It wasn't that bad," he assures in a raspy, weak voice walking unsteadily past those getting in line to ride. "I'm glad we rode it," he pushes out.

I grab his arm and pull him back towards the line, asking, "So, you wanna go again?"

"Nah. Once is good enough."

"Are you sure?" I tease. "The line's right there."

"No, okay?" I just laugh and we keep walking.

We pass the twenty-foot-tall statue of Loggie, the park's namesake. He looks like a retro cartoon figure with bleach blond spiky hair, a dark blue, long-sleeved shirt, red parachute pants, and black tennis shoes. I think what I like the most is the goofy smile on his face as he looks out towards the horizon.

Nearby, we see a line of vendor stands. Chet turns to me and points at a nearby wooden bench, saying, "You sit here in the shade. I'll be right back."

"Okay."

He returns a few minutes later, and a warm feeling bubbles up within me as I see what he has. "Cotton candy!" I squeal like a little girl. "I *love* cotton candy!"

He grins happily. "Well, here you go," he says as he hands one to me. "I got us some fruit slushies, too."

"Thanks, Chet!" I gush. "I haven't had this since I was, like, four," I exaggerate. He sets the slushie cup down beside me.

I tear off a strand of blue and pink and pop it in my mouth. It's super sweet and I relish how it just melts away. "My dad loved it. He introduced me and now, I love it, too! Good memories."

"Did your mom like it, too?"

I shrug. "Not really."

"You don't talk much about your folks," he says, eating his cotton candy like a turkey leg.

"It's sensitive," I reply. They've been divorced for almost ten years. "I'm careful with it, I guess."

By the time I finish my cotton candy, Chet's about halfway through his. He's been people watching while I've enjoyed looking at him. He's tall compared to me with a build like a soccer player. He's not an athlete, though; he stays busy doing odd jobs. He turns to check on me and I catch his dreamy brown eyes as he smiles.

"So, what do you wanna do next?" he asks.

"Wait. Let me ask you something."

"Sure."

"Do you believe in soulmates?"

He's still smiling, but I see confusion in his face. "I don't know. Do you?"

"I'd like to," I reply with a cautious smile. "I've watched older couples sometimes and it's obvious they've been together for a long time with the way they move and talk, the looks they give each other."

"How they finish each other's sentences or kinda look alike," he adds.

"Yeah," I say, taking a second to think about it. "I wonder how they stay like that?"

He gives me another confused look. "Dunno. Are you thinkin' about us like that? Because —"

"No," I interrupt, embarrassed. I don't want to scare him away with any more "soulmate" talk. "I was just talking." This feels so awkward. "Your folks are still married, right?"

"Yep. Twenty-seven years," he replies proudly.

"Sometimes I wish my parents were still married," I tell him. "But Dad cheated on Mom, and she divorced him."

I can tell he doesn't know what to say now. *That's enough,* I tell myself. *No more sad stuff.* "Sorry."

"Let's go grab some pizza and soda," he suggests and I'm glad he does. "Really, I don't mind talking about stuff, and you can ask me whatever you want. Deal?"

"Yeah, let's go."

•••

"What's your favorite color?" I ask while we wait on our medium "LoggieWorks" pizza. We're sitting on a bench seat with a blue canopy overhead, our large styrofoam cups of Dr. Cola placed on the park table.

"Turquoise," he replies.

"Seriously?" I wonder, surprised. "Turquoise?"

"It's a *real* color, and I like it," he says with a slight edge.

What, did I hurt his feelings? "Dude, chill. It's just a question."

"I know," he says, relaxing. "Can I ask your race? It's not a big deal, but I wanna know."

Why should that matter to him? It's making my stomach tighten. *It's a simple question,* I tell myself. *Just answer it.* "I'm a quarter Chinese," I relent. "The rest is German, Scottish, and Irish."

"Wow! That's really interesting!" he replies enthusiastically.

That makes me blush. "You think so? Why?"

He shrugs. "I don't think I've known anyone with that mix of races before."

That makes me chuckle. "You probably have and didn't know it. It's pretty common."

"Ninety-Seven!" the male cashier shouts from the food truck.

Chet goes to get our pizza, and I think about how to change the subject. Stuff about my family isn't a favorite topic. When Chet returns with the box, I ask, "Can we take this to the hotel? We can come back tomorrow."

"Yeah, that works."

•••

We head back to the St. Louis Edevane Hotel in our rental car. The ten-story building is a couple of miles from the park. It's not super-posh but it's what we could afford for this three-day vacation. Our suite starts with a small hallway that leads into a medium-sized bedroom. The bathroom with a shower is tucked into one corner of the suite. But it's more than enough for our needs.

Chet and I have been dating for two months and he's already pretty good at picking up on my little hints. There are only two reasons I'd want to leave the park and go back to the hotel before dark: I've had enough of the scenery, and I want him. By the time we're in our room, we're both in the mood. I leave the Do Not Disturb sign hanging on the outside handle and lock the door. The blinds are closed for privacy but there's enough twilight sun seeping through for what we need. Seconds later, we're making out against one wall.

"You brought protection, right?" I ask breathily between kisses.

"Yeah, in my suitcase," he says with eyes half-closed. "Just give me a minute."

"Okay, but *only* a minute," I tease.

He practically throws open his suitcase and flies through its contents. Then he stops and gives me a strange glance. "They're not in here. I think I forgot the condoms."

Seriously? He realizes this now?

"I can either go get some or we can just keep going." His face is extremely serious. I know he wants me right now. I want him, too. But the risk?

I see his expression start to change. He's disappointed, and he starts walking towards the door. "I'm going."

I'm taking too long. I don't want him to lose interest in me! I *won't* let that happen.

"Baby," I say in my most alluring voice. He turns his head toward me and sees me slowly begin to remove my tee shirt. With a come-hither look, I say, "You're not going anywhere."

•••

I wake up and quietly check the time on the nightstand's digital alarm clock, the room's only light source. It's 11:57 p.m. Through the window, I can hear cars drive by below and a few people walking down the hallway past our door. The cool breeze from the A.C. feels nice. Looking at Chet's silhouette next to me on the bed, his light snore lets me know he's still asleep. Thinking about him brings a smile to my face. It was so good. *He* was so good! I close my eyes and relive it a few times, grinning. Does that mean I love him?

There's a light tapping against the window. It's raining? That's nice. It'll relax me back to sleep.

Another thought tugs at me and I open my eyes with a new worry: What if Chet and I just made a baby? Did I really think our relationship would end if we didn't have sex right then? But we've always used protection before.

I squint my eyes, wanting to bat all this away like a bad dream. It was just one time.

Outside, it's raining harder now. Stop overthinking about this. It's not that big a deal. If I don't think it happened, then it didn't happen. I'm not going to get pregnant. It was just one time.

Now I relax some. My mind starts to drift but before everything fades, one last thought occurs to me, but I choose to ignore it:

It only takes one time.

2

11:48 A.M. MONDAY JULY 22ND – GZELLE COMPUTERS – OVERLAND PARK, KANSAS

I pick up the Haverson Project report from the printer and head back to my desk. As soon as I sit down, I set it to one side and review an email for an upcoming Gzelle event we're planning. I just want to make sure which teams are participating.

"Wanna join us for lunch, Julie? Me and Suzie are going to DFC."

I force my attention away from my work laptop to look at my tall and heavyset manager, Rachel, who just gave the invite. Turning my head towards the window, it's sunny and clear outside. And I've had lunch with them before; they usually just talk about their husbands and kids, but it's better than eating alone. Still, do I really want fried chicken? Before I can answer her, I get a text notification. "One second, Rachel," I reply, looking down at my phone. "It's from Chet."

Chet: Free for a picnic lunch? I made sandwiches and grabbed some sodas.

Me: Your timing's perfect! Yes, I'm free.

Chet: Be there in 5. Meet me out front.

Me: Deal.

I don't want to be a jerk towards my coworkers but Chet's my guy. "Sorry, Rachel. He made a picnic lunch for us, and he's on his way here. Another time?"

"Sure, Julie."

Suzie nods and winks at me. "Have a great lunch with that guy you stole from me!" We all laugh. I almost forgot they were there when I first met Chet.

I wave at them and then go spend a few minutes freshening up in the ladies' room. Why did I choose this blouse today? It looks too small on me. "I better not be pregnant, I better not be pregnant," I mutter to myself, fighting back fear. Anyway, I can't do anything about that now. Hopefully, Chet won't notice. As soon as I've finished straightening out my hair, I head out front. Chet's waiting for me in his used white Camaro with classic rock music booming.

When he sees me, he gets out and holds open the passenger door.

"You didn't have to do that," I say, though I'm glad he did.

"I wanna do that for my lady," he says with an adorable shrug as I get in. He gently closes the door and returns to the driver's seat, turning down the music.

I'm already in a better mood just being near him. "What's lunch?" I ask playfully.

"Sandwiches from my catering job," he replies. "I did some deliveries for them this morning, so they let me make this picnic lunch before I left."

"Nice! What kind of sandwiches?"

"Ham, turkey, and Colby Jack," he replies smoothly. "With some lettuce, tomato, and red onions. I grabbed some spicy brown mustard for you."

"Thanks, babe!" My fingers are tapping to the melody on my armrest.

"You're welcome," he says cheerily.

We drive a few miles to the park. Then we stroll towards the wooden tables with benches. It feels nice to walk hand-in-hand with Chet. I watch the warm breeze ruffling his hair and imagine my fingers doing the same. The adoring way he looks at me is intoxicating and I almost forget where we are. A glance to my right reveals the grass and trees, so lush and green from some recent rain. Joggers and a few families are taking advantage of the pleasant weather.

"I would've gotten us a blanket so we could sit on the ground, but I didn't have time," he says, regaining my full attention.

"That's alright," I assure him. "I'm fine with a table."

We sit down, and he opens the basket, pulling out two red and white checkered plates. Then he sets a paper-wrapped sandwich on each plate followed by a bag of potato chips. He places one in front of me and gives me a can of Dr. Cola. "Enjoy," he says.

"I'm sure I will!" I unwrap my sandwich, pull open the chips bag, and pop the tab on the soda. I take a bite of the sandwich. The meat is juicy, the cheese is high quality, and the veggies are so fresh! I look at him and say, "My co-workers were gonna take me to DFC, but I definitely got the better deal. This is delicious!"

He nods and asks, "What's been going on with you?"

I shrug. "Nothing special. Work keeps me busy." I have some of the chips and drink some soda. "End of month reports and stuff like that. At home, I've been working on a new song."

"Really? Can I hear it?" he wonders. "I don't get to hear you play much."

"Um, sure," I reply nervously. "I'm just, um, not used to playing for others."

"Even if It's just me?"

I feel my cheeks warm. "Okay. Just for you." He grins. I pull out my phone and go to an audio recording I made of my song. "Sorry about the sound quality. It was supposed to be just for me."

"That's okay."

I'm still nervous as I start playing the recording. After a few seconds, he closes his eyes and slowly bobs his head to the rhythm of the piano. Not long after that, he opens his eyes and asks, "Is that you singing?"

I forgot that I sang along with the notes in this recording. There's no lyrics but the melody made me want to harmonize with it. I didn't know I'd be playing it for Chet.

"Yeah," I admit, still nervous.

"You have a pretty voice."

"Thanks."

The recording finishes not long after that. "I just wanted to get the main melody and a few chord changes," I tell him. "That's not the full song."

"Well, it's pretty," he remarks. "And I like it. Thanks for letting me hear it."

"Sure, babe."

"I'm gonna have a booth at the crafts show downtime this Saturday," he says. "Wanna come along and keep me company?"

Chet has a hobby of carving wooden animals, especially ducks and other waterfowl, and painting them to look realistic. He makes them on the days he's not working. He started doing this in his early teens and now they're high enough quality that he can sell them for a decent price. "Yeah, I'll come along."

He gives me a big smile and says, "Thanks. That'll help me a whole lot."

"It'll be fun," I suggest.

We finish our food over the next few minutes in silence. I still have butterflies in my stomach from his charm and being able to share my music with him. Being in this place with him makes me feel special. It's so sweet.

"You brought all this, let me pack it up for you," I offer.

"Okay," he says, finishing his drink. "Thanks."

It doesn't take long to clean up the table and put everything away before heading back to his car.

"I don't know how you do it, but you keep getting better looking all the time, Julie," he says while gazing at my chest.

Crud! He noticed my blouse after all! Completely embarrassing. "Um, thank you," I reply nervously. "Sorry, I meant to have a looser blouse on."

"It's okay, it's great" he says, slowly shaking his head as he continues to gaze at my chest and smile.

It brings about a rush of emotions in me. I'm glad he thinks I'm sexy but at the same time, I'm so scared that these changes are proof I really *am* pregnant. And that's overwhelming. I don't want a baby! Fortunately, the ride to work is smooth and talking about normal things relaxes me.

"I'll text you later," I tell him as we arrive. "Thanks again for lunch."

"Sure," he replies.

I go inside and clock in right at one o'clock.

"How's my guy?" Suzie jokes as I sit back down at my desk that faces hers.

Before I can joke back at her, I feel a rush of nausea zoom up from my belly. "He's good, he's good! `Scuse me," I whimper as I quickly leave the work area to head to the restroom. Seriously? Am I getting morning sickness now? What is happening to me? I spend the next five minutes literally losing my lunch. I feel spent and shocked.

I hear someone enter the bathroom. "Julie, you okay, `hon?" Suzie asks.

"Getting there," I whimper back. Then I puke some more.

"Oh, my gosh! What did you eat?" Suzie gasps. "Do I need to get the nurse?" she asks in a hushed voice.

"No," I answer.

"Let me know if you need anything," she adds.

I can't respond. I'm still catching my breath.

After I finish cleaning up, I look at myself in the bathroom mirror, confirming once again how my breasts have gotten larger.

Then it all starts to hit. They're actually sore. Oh, no! They're actually sore! And I just emptied my whole stomach out. What other signs are there?

There's no question now: I've *got* to take a pregnancy test!

•••

THE NEXT MORNING

I've never felt like this. And I think my piano is the only thing that can bring me solace right now. I sit down, open the lid and spread my fingers over the keys. The piano listens to my innermost feelings and lets me express them through notes and chords. The music we make together conveys who I am and helps me laugh or cry or rage, and I always feel better afterwards. I really need it today.

I'm still working on my new song. I haven't named it yet, but it's light and airy. It's still untitled, but I might call it "Hope" or "Chasing the Sunrise" because as it progresses, it reminds me of a young girl running through a field of flowers in the morning light. It's how I want to feel. My playing slows as reality invades my fantasy.

I took three different pregnancy tests half an hour ago. And they're all positive. Seeing those little double pink lines staring back at me makes this real. And if Chet could see how my body's changing, Mom will, too.

Fear leads my fingers to brush across the keys and begin playing Rachmaninoff: Piano Concerto no.2 op.18. Its beautiful dreariness matches how I really feel. I'm not a little girl and I'm not running through a pretty field towards a hopeful sunrise. I'm stuck. With a sharp inhale, I make myself focus on the keys instead of my stomach. In my mind, an orchestra accompanies me. The music lets me escape for seconds at a time.

My glasses start to slip down my nose, distracting me from my distraction. I force myself to keep playing and shake my head in denial. It causes my hair to bounce against each side of my face. I don't want to cry but a tear runs down my cheek anyway.

"You're up early."

I wipe the tear away quickly. It's Mom.

Look at how she glides down the stairs with one hand gracing the winding metal rails. From her long, wavy, eternally black hair parted in the middle to her tan, long-sleeved blouse and those bell bottom-esque olive slacks with low heel black dress shoes, she makes forty-eight look like the pinnacle of modern beauty. And she's only a lawyer.

I'm not ready for cross-examination with Mom right now; I'm too emotional. I need to act like nothing's wrong. Yeahhhhh, right. I gotta say as little as possible. "I felt like playing this morning."

"Your skill with the piano has truly evolved over the years," she pitches as she crosses the living room into the kitchen. "Have you considered teaching piano or playing professionally?"

I wish I'd gotten more sleep. "Thanks," I offer. "I don't think I'm good enough to teach, much less play professionally. And I'm still happy with my job at Gzelle."

I guess she can't help but turn up her nose at my comment. "As an administrative planner at a two-bit computer company? All you do is word processing and make spreadsheets for sales teams...for fifteen dollars an hour at that," she scoffs.

Don't get mad. Stay calm. "Could I make more than that teaching piano to teenagers?" I counter.

Her smile let me know she wasn't hearing me. "With the children of my clients, I'd get you at least *double* that. Maybe triple."

"Well, no, thank you," I say, matching her tone. "Like I said, I'm not ready for that yet."

She pauses to look at me, but I'm not budging on this. Finally, she sighs. "Let me know if you change your mind," she says with a pleasant air. That's her way of not giving up, either. "Or get fed up with your job."

"Alright."

"Also, bring your umbrella to work today. It's going to thunderstorm," she adds before walking over to me. I stand up and face her respectfully. "I love you," she says, kissing me on the cheek. "See you tonight."

"Love you, too, Mom. See you tonight."

I watch her walk out the front door. My heart pounds as I hear the BMW start up. I grip my arms, close my eyes and endure the eternity it takes for the sounds of her car to fade with distance. Then I go to the front window and pull the curtain back to actually verify she's gone. This is serious! She may not know yet, but it's only gonna get harder to hide this from her. I start to pace across the living room. If I can't hide it, that means I'll have to tell her. I'm not ready for that! I'm not ready for that...

At times like now, when I need a hug, I go to Mom's room. Kind of like when I was little. And as I slowly head up the stairs, I feel like I'm sleepwalking.

Opening her door, it's as if I've entered a forest in winter with a large, elegant bed at its center and a clear crystal chandelier acting as the sun above it. It's gorgeous but I've never liked it; it doesn't match the rest of the house. The wallpaper behind the bed is scary: white oak trees against a black background. She once told me the white bed covered in black and white-striped sheets is supposed to look like snow-covered dark soil and the silken black and silver pillows laying against the headboard represent smooth stones on more snow. I can picture it but it's still dull and depressing to me. Just like the dark curtains over blinds, three gray walls, pale ceiling, and black-tiled floor. All of it makes me ache for her, it's so sad! Even her dual-shelved bookcase with her collections of glass-enclosed orchids makes me feel trapped as I look at them.

This reflects her. It's her sanctuary. And it's so different from the Mom she used to be.

In my mind, I can see this room through my ten-year-old eyes. The bed wasn't fancy, but it was soft and fun to bounce up and down on. There was a ceiling fan I would watch until I got dizzy. No chandelier, just a white round cover over a simple lightbulb. There were framed paintings of birds and ducks on the bright blue walls. And it had thick, shaggy blue carpet I adored. I would scoot across it in my shorts just to feel it against my knees.

The room wasn't pristine like it is now. Mom would leave clothes on the floor and half the bed would stay unmade. She'd let me get in bed with her on the weekends if Dad was at work. Her hair might be in simple braids or kinda messy, and she wore simple, loose-fitting clothes, but I didn't care; I was looking at her big smile and pretty brown eyes. We'd play in here for hours at a time.

She and Dad were happy, and they made me happy.

Looking around the room as it is now, I wish Mom could be the way she was back then. I know *that* Mom would accept me. She'd help me decide what to do about this pregnancy, and I wouldn't be scared.

I just know I can't keep procrastinating. Walking downstairs slowly, I run my hand along my stomach. "People say you're just a clump of cells," I tell my kid. "But if that's true, why are you affecting my body so much already?"

I sit down on the couch and use my phone to look up pregnancy care. If I'm having this baby, let's see what's involved. My mini-research session shows me the need for an OBGYN, taking "maternal vitamins," cutting down my caffeine, and eating healthier. I can do that, right? I mean...right?

•••

My barbarian chick smashes a fourth desert goblin with her splintered hinwood club. Her armor's almost broken and she needs some more health potion bottles. Another hour and I might just make it out of this dungeon. It's pretty cool that I've gotten this far in *Eternal Delusion XLIX*, especially playing solo. Things would go faster with a team, but I don't want the drama from other players. The snack plate next to me has fig jelly with thin crackers. They go really well with the ginger and carrot juice in my travel mug. It's really helping with my nausea.

Next to the mouse, my phone lights up with a text message from Chet.

Chet: You free tonight?

Me: Maybe. :)

Chet: Wanna see a movie?

Me: Which one?

Chet: How about "*Keys to Wonder*?" It's about a female piano player.

He's so sweet.

Me: Okay, that sounds good. When?

Chet: There's a showing at eight.

Me: Perfect!

Chet: I'll call you when I'm on the way.

He's always so kind to me. Things like this make me want to tell him about the pregnancy and wonder what kind of dad he'd be. If we had a daughter, I imagine he'd be so protective towards her, and she'd adore him like I do. And if we had a son, I could see them going everywhere together.

I close my eyes and wrap my arms around my stomach, allowing myself to feel warm and happy... even if it's just for this moment.

Then I look at the clock on my phone and see that fifteen minutes has zoomed by. I need to get ready.

3

11:16 P.M. WEDNESDAY JULY 31st – CHET'S APARTMENT

When I wake, it takes me a few seconds to remember where I am. I turn and see Chet next to me on his bed. He sleeps so soundly. I did, too, for a while. The lamp by the bed is still on and the A/C is blowing pretty loudly. I look at Chet again. I'd like to run my hand through his hair and kiss his handsome face some more, but I don't want to wake him. With all I've been going through in the last couple of weeks, I really needed him tonight.

Quietly, I slip out of bed and hunt for my clothes on the dark carpeted floor.

But I instantly startle when I hear his drowsy voice say, "Everything okay, babe?"

"Yeah. Sorry to wake you."

"S'okay," he mumbles. "You leavin' already?"

"It's pretty late," I say as I start getting dressed. I'll shower when I get home.

"Stay a little longer, okay? Talk with me."

"You want to talk?" I ask, surprised.

"I've noticed you've been kinda down lately," he replies, now resting on one elbow. "Wanna talk about it?"

"Chet, I love...being with you, being your girlfriend," I say as I button my blouse. My heart is already beating faster. "I guess I've...been wondering about us, about our future. So, tell me, where do you see things going?"

He looks at me with those tender eyes of his and I see him thinking about his answer. His smile gives me hope.

"I love being with you, too, Julie. I'm glad we're together," he says honestly. His tone lowers softly. "We have so much fun, I haven't thought much about the future. I'm happy where we are. I want us to hold onto this for as long as we can. Is that alright?"

"What does that mean?" I ask, confused by his vague answer. "That doesn't tell me anything."

"This," he answers. "Being boyfriend and girlfriend."

Wrong answer. "*This* is all you want us to be?" I reply angrily. "Like forever?"

"Well, not forever," he says defensively, sitting up, still covered by the sheet.

I put my hands on my hips and huff, "How long then? Six months? Six *years?* Am I just gonna be your 'fun lover' and that's it?" I'm getting so frustrated, I can't shut myself up. "Have you ever thought *I* might want more than that?"

"You do?" he counters. "You haven't said anything till now."

"Did I *have* to? I —!" Suddenly, I have to stop. A huge wave of nausea rises in my stomach, and it takes all my strength not to throw up right there. I can feel my chest heave, and he's looking right at me. I try to make it look like a sigh as I hold my hand up. "Y'know what? I'm going."

"Hey," he says, sounding disappointed.

I shake my head, grab my purse, and head towards the front door. "Don't follow me," I insist, barely able to speak. Then I close the door behind me and rush downstairs towards my car. I finally vomit on a grass patch by the sidewalk. It takes a while to calm down and get my strength back. I'm glad Chet didn't get dressed and come after me. I'm still lightheaded but as soon as I feel like I can drive, I leave and don't look back.

Ew! I smell so gross. I want to rinse and spit and wash up.

At the same time, my mind replays Chet's words over and over. I wish I'd known this before we went to the amusement park!

I pass by the businesses, other vehicles, and the few people out, but it's like I'm still in Chet's apartment face-to-face with him. Why is he like this? I want to call him and ask, "How can you know me so well but not see us going deeper in this relationship?" But I'm scared. I don't think I wanna know his answer.

Pulling up to a blinking red light at an intersection, I ease to a stop.

"I'm happy where we are," his words repeat in my mind. "I want us to hold onto this for as long as we can. Is that alright?"

No, Chet. That's *not* alright! I'm pregnant. We can't just float around in "Happyville" forever.

A driver behind me honks their horn obnoxiously. I make sure the intersection's safe and pull forward. I'm not ready to deal with Chet. I'll give him some space and make him think I'm angry at him.

Then I bang my fist on the steering wheel. How can I be mad at Chet when I refuse to tell him about my pregnancy? This is stupid! I should turn around and go tell him right now!

But I don't. I keep driving until I reach my street and turn onto it.

Because I'm too scared to lose him.

•••

Most of my nausea is gone by the time I get home. I expect Mom to be in bed by now. But she's fallen asleep on the couch, and her laptop has her latest case information displayed atop the coffee table. She's still in her work clothes and the kitchen and lamp lights are both on. Despite my poor mood, I feel bad for her. She works too hard.

I slip by the couch and go to use the bathroom. Then I brush my teeth and take a quick shower before returning to wake her. "Mom, I'm home," I say softly. "You shouldn't sleep out here."

It takes a few seconds for her to stir and open her eyes. She yawns and deflects with, "I've worked till sunup for years. Don't worry."

"You know it's bad for your posture and you'll get a crick in your neck," I counter. "Let me help you to your room."

"What time is it?" she murmurs.

"A little after midnight."

"You're just getting home? Good date with Chet?"

I'm not gonna answer that. Instead, I help her stand up. "I'll shut off your laptop in a minute," I tell her. "Do you need any of the files saved?"

We start walking towards the stairs. "No. I was just reading some documents." Her voice sounds so tired. She doesn't even look towards the computer as she says it and she has a resentful expression. Is her career starting to burn her out?

As Mom starts changing into a nightgown, I stand against the doorway and gaze towards the stairs. When I hear her get into bed, I go over and attempt to cover her with the blanket, but she weakly pushes my hand away. "G'night," she mumbles.

"Good night, Mom," I say with a trembling voice. I back away slowly, putting my hand to my chest.

I really wanted to talk to her. I *needed* to talk to her...but she won't let me. I'm really alone.

Her eyes are already closed and she's almost asleep. Before I leave, I make sure her bedside alarm clock is set. She'll have a seizure if she oversleeps, especially if she has to be in court tomorrow.

It's so obvious to me. This woman's not happy. Whatever her career has been, it's not doing it for her anymore. And she won't accept help...even from me. How can we get close like we used to be if this is where we are? Walking back downstairs, I shut down Mom's laptop and plug it into its charger cable, so it'll be ready for her in the morning. Sitting down on the couch, my thoughts keep racing.

I place my hand on my stomach, thinking about this tiny baby inside me. Right now, I feel stuck...but am I really? Chet just wants a girlfriend, and Mom wants a career daughter. All of my worrying about reaching out to Mom and telling Chet, but I don't have to tell anyone. I could have an abortion. Women get them all the time. So, if it isn't a big deal to them, it doesn't need to be a big deal to me. I could call the Sanger Center tomorrow. They say they help pregnant women. "I'll ask for information, that's all," I tell myself. "Yeah, I can do that." I find their phone number online and add it to my contacts.

•••

6:00 P.M. THE NEXT DAY

"I've *got* to tell him." The Gzelle building grows smaller in my rearview mirror as I increase my speed. At first, I'm heading home but my thoughts are all about Chet. About our baby. And how my visit at the Sanger Center went this morning.

The middle-aged blonde I talked to in private was named Marcy. "Your pregnancy test came back positive," she'd said politely from behind her desk. "Based on your information, you appear to be about ten or eleven weeks pregnant."

"Really?" I'd asked with wide eyes.

"Yes," she'd answered.

I was further along than I thought.

Instead of going north on the freeway, I head south to see Chet.

Maybe he'll talk me out of it.

"Will the baby feel anything?" I'd asked Marcy. "You know, from the abortion?"

Marcy shook her head and smiled. "No, Julie. The fetus is basically just a clump of cells at this stage. It can't feel anything," she'd assured me. "The important thing is that if you want to end your pregnancy, it's best to do so in the first trimester."

"How big is the fetus right now?" I'd asked, putting a hand on my belly.

She'd paused to think before replying, "About two to three inches long," she said. "Maybe the size of a plum."

That made me tense up. "That sounds like *more* than just a clump of cells," I grumbled.

"Would you like to hear more about this procedure? It's simple and you can be done in just one visit," Marcy had replied soothingly.

The cars in front of me slow down and stop. There are so many of them, it's gonna take forever to get to Chet's. I think about calling or texting him, but what can I say over the phone? This is too big.

I'd felt so much pressure sitting there in Marcy's office. She was patient with me, but I was torn about making the decision. I'd felt cold and clammy, and every second was an eternity. No matter what I decided, I wasn't going to be happy.

Finally, traffic starts moving again and I make it to the right exit. I haven't been in the mood for music. I'm so sad. I don't want to do this! Chet, help me! I want to tell you about this baby so bad. I turn into his neighborhood, feeling my tears streaming down my cheeks. I need you, Chet. Would you do this with me? Will you love me and raise this kid with me?

I was starting to feel claustrophobic in Marcy's office. I had to decide. And I wanted my life back. "Alright," I told her. "Set it up."

"I have a 1:30 P.M. appointment this Friday afternoon," Marcy answered. "How does that sound?"

It sounded terrible. But it was my way out of this mess. "Sure."

I've been idling, parked along the curb in front of a stranger's house, for a couple of minutes already. I can't go any further. Feelings and images flood my being.

Luring Chet to me in the hotel room, terrified of losing the moment. Choosing bliss, a massive high followed by the lowest low as I reach out to him from a distance now. He can't see me at the bottom of this ditch.

And I remember Dad walking out the front door with two suitcases as Mom cursed him out.

Back to Chet telling me he's happy being my boyfriend. Don't think about the future.

Seeing Mom passed out on the couch looking miserable.

Staring at the positive pregnancy test. Always in the bathroom, either using the toilet or puking into it. A baby!

It's a clump of cells. Get rid of it! You can keep things like they are with Chet.

I don't want to!

What *do* I want?

I don't want to be alone! I don't want to lose you, Chet!

I can't lose you! I can't lose anything else!

What about the baby? Can you lose him or her?

It. It's just a clump of cells. It can't feel anything...it can't feel anything.

The baby or Chet. I can't have both. He'll leave me. He doesn't want things to change.

This is my fault. I did all this. I have to fix it.

I sit there and cry for a while, cold sweat lining my brow and back. I drink some more of my bottled fruit juice, wishing it was a Dr. Cola. My snack bag is in the passenger seat but all I want is sausage pizza. As much as I want to go to Chet, I can't. I know what I have to do now. Instead of taking a right onto Chet's street, I slowly turn around and head in the opposite direction. I'm committed. And two days from now, it'll be over.

4

5:23 P.M. THURSDAY AUGUST 1st – THE CONVENIENT MART

I barely made it through the workday. I'm so munchie hungry! I take my car to the closest convenience store. There aren't any parking spots right in front of the building, so I park next to the dumpster. The sign next to it reads "No Parking Zone" but whatever. I lock the car and go inside the store. The candy aisle has so many colorful packages. I grab two king-sized chocolate bars. They still make grape dinosaur gummies? Yeah, I'm snatching that. I fill a bakery bag with two chocolate covered donuts and a glazed one, just to even it out. The candy can wait till tomorrow, but the donuts will go stale if I don't eat them tonight.

Before I can grab anything else, I hear the tingling of piano keys from my phone. It's a text from Dad!

Dad: Hey pumpkin

Me: What's up dad?

Dad: Want to have dinner with us tonight?

Me: Is it a special occasion or something?

Dad: Kind of. Mostly, Bao and your little sisters want to see you. It's been a while.

That's because every time I go to see them, it drives Mom insane for a week. But whatever, I miss them, too.

Me: Okay. When?

Dad: Can you make it by 7? Bao is cooking tonight.

Okay, that seals the deal. She's a great cook!

Me: Sure. I'll be there.

Dad: K then! Love you kiddo!

Me: Love you too

After I take a second to think about it, I facepalm. Why did I just say I'd eat with them tonight with what's going on? The abortion may be tomorrow, but Bao might notice stuff when she sees me; she's been pregnant twice. Heck, my sisters might notice how big my breasts have gotten and ask about it. Really loudly.

Oh, crud! How long have I been standing here in the store just thinking? I need to get back to my car. I go to the cashier to pay for my munchies then hurry outside and look towards the dumpster.

Where's my car?

My gaze darts all around the parking lot. No car. I see something in the corner of my eye and spin around. There's my little orange Toyota zooming away. It's fastened to a tow truck! There's no way I can flag them down now.

I have once again proven to myself that I'm an idiot. A car-less, pregnant idiot.

"Was that your car?" a little boy says a few feet away. He's with a man — his father, I guess — and pointing towards the tow truck. "I told them not to take it." He looks at his father. "Didn't I, Dad?"

"You did," he agrees and then looks at me. "But the man was just doing his job. People aren't supposed to park in those spots."

Thanks, mister. Like rubbing it in helps. I just watch as they get in their SUV and leave. He's right, though. It was stupid to park there.

I *really* don't want to call and beg Chet for a ride. Wait! I'm having dinner with Dad anyway. I'll call him instead.

•••

I'm glad to see Dad pull up to the convenience store in his shiny red Voltaic car. I was starting to get tired and uncomfortable leaning against the front wall of the building, especially with it starting to get dark. It looks like he came straight from work. He and Mom are both so stylish. Look at him: always clean-shaven, keeping his brown hair so trim and slicked back. His tailored dark blue suit looks like it cost what I make in a week. But he's the Marketing Vice-President of Delusory Insurance; he can afford it. I've always admired his professional drive. He and Mom both have it, and I totally don't.

I stand here like a lost puppy with my snack bags in my right hand and my bindle purse set on my other shoulder. "I really messed up, Dad," I say, embarrassed. "I'm sorry. Thanks for coming."

"It's alright, Pumpkin." He smiles at me. "I'm just glad I can help."

I look at the ground, still ashamed. "I can't believe this."

"Do you have the towing company's contact information?" he asks.

"Yeah. They had a little business sign with their number on the convenience store wall next to the window."

Dad opens the passenger side door for me. "Good. We'll go there tomorrow and get your car back."

I get in and start fastening the seatbelt. "Can we do that on Saturday? I have work and a...doctor's appointment at one-thirty tomorrow."

He closes the door and continues talking once he's in the driver's seat. "How are you going to get there? And are you alright?"

"I'll take a PayMeRide," I answer. "And it's just a yearly checkup."

"Oh, okay." He takes a breath and gives me a concerned look. But then he releases it and faces forward. Does he not believe me? Maybe I shouldn't have done this. I should've just canceled for dinner and got a PayMeRide home. Now what's gonna happen?

"Don't worry about the cost of getting your car back," he finally says. "I'll cover it."

"No," I blurt with wide eyes as I turn to face him, putting my hand on his arm. "I plan to do it. It's okay."

He gives me a charming smile. "C'mon, don't deny your dad the chance to be your knight in shining armor!" It's so sweet and so corny. Very Dad.

"Alright," I reply, forcing a chuckle. Part of me wants to cry, though. I'm such a loser. I still need to be "rescued by daddy."

"We all make mistakes, Julie," he says as he starts up the car. "They all have consequences...some more than others. Getting your car out of the tow lot isn't that bad."

"Yeah."

It takes the whole fifteen-minute drive for me to plan out what I'm going to say during this visit. When we get to his two-story house in the Colonial Village neighborhood, I look at the Cherrybark Oak tree in their front yard. I remember when they first moved in, it was so tiny. But now it's grown like their family. And Bao built up their colorful flower garden from scratch next to the front door. The look of it is so soothing. Dad pulls into the driveway next to Bao's blue SUV and parks. It's a pretty house, not too posh; it just says "family" to me.

And I have to admit, I envy their life. They're always doing things together like going to the park and little vacations. My favorite place to go was the State Fair, back when we were the family — Dad, me, and Mom. Now, I'm either alone all the time or hearing Mom's bitter take on life. Sometimes, I wish Dad had gotten custody of me. But then, I'd feel worse for Mom.

Dad unlocks the front door, and Bao meets us in the hallway almost immediately. She gives him a quick kiss and then turns to me with a wide grin and open arms. "Julie! It's so good to see you!" We hug for a couple of seconds. She's wearing that rose petal perfume again.

"I'm really glad you could make it. Your sisters have been asking about you."

As she pulls back, still smiling, I admire her denim skirt with an elegant light blue blouse. She's a fit woman but she's gained a few pounds since I last saw her. Her black hair is pulled back into a cute, long ponytail.

"I've missed them, too," I tell her honestly. "How are they doing?"

"Well, Hua has made a lot of friends at school," she begins. "And Chow can't decide whether she loves or hates her preschool class."

I smile as I say, "Mom told me I didn't like preschool, either. Or kindergarten. But apparently, I got used to school by the second grade." To her credit, Bao never seems uncomfortable when I mention Mom.

She nods as the three of us walk towards the living room. "Hua was the same way. It's kind of strange, since I loved school, from what I remember," she says before glancing at Dad who's walking ahead of us. "They must have gotten that rebellious streak from *you*, John."

He chuckles from the living room where he's already loosening his tie. "Yeah, I hated school all around."

"Then how did you manage to stay in till you got a master's degree in business?" she jokes.

"I may've hated school, but I needed the degree," he answers, sitting down in a recliner.

"And he worked hard for it," Bao boasts.

It feels weird to hear this about Dad's history from Bao instead of Mom. Then again, Mom would've found some way to belittle him about it.

"Julie's here!" Hua cries out from her room's open doorway as soon as she sees me.

Her little sister runs to her side to see, eyes full of joy. "Julie!"

Now it's my turn to open my arms. They're both a little chubby and have Dad's eyes with Bao's hair. They're so adorable. I scoop Chow up in my arms. "You've gotten taller!"

"Yup!" she nods happily.

"Are you still dating that 'Chat' guy?" Hua asks, looking very curious.

Whoa! That came out of nowhere. Then again, Chet did come with me when I visited them last month. It surprised me how well they got along when they played together.

I laugh a little to hide how nervous that question made me. "Chet," I correct. "And yes, I'm still dating him."

Chet's really good with kids.

"You gonna marry him?" Hua asks innocently.

He's good with kids...but I'm planning to... "I don't know," I tell her. I start to move my hand towards my stomach but stop myself. That was close!

Bao decides to come to my rescue. "Everyone, come to the table!" She's wearing oven mitts now and setting down the casserole dish at the table's center.

Chow, who's still in my arms, leans closer and loudly whispers, "Mommy's gonna give us a brudder or sister!" I give Chow an exaggerated blink and try to look happily surprised instead of the mild shock I'm really feeling.

Now Bao blushes. "We were going to tell you during the meal, Julie, but it's true. You're going to have another sibling."

Great. This dinner just turned awkward.

"Congratulations" I tell Bao, trying to fake being enthusiastic. I make myself go over to her, still holding Chow in one arm, and give her another hug but I'm getting overwhelmed. I set Chow down but feel lightheaded standing back up.

Though I'm trying to look fine, Dad asks, "Julie, what's wrong?" When I glance at him, he looks worried.

"What? I'm fine," I reply lightly. He frowns and keeps looking at me. Yeah, he knows something's up. "This was just a surprise. But really, I'm happy about it."

"Are you worried about how your mom's going to react?" he adds.

He guessed the wrong thing! Thanks for giving me an out, Dad. You're the best! "You know Mom."

Bao loses her smile, but she doesn't look upset. Dad looks like he understands. He's not pleased, either. "Jocelyn needs to let go," he says wearily, maintaining eye contact with me. "She's been clinging onto me for a decade and all she's done is hurt herself." And me. "She's pushing herself to an early grave."

Bao gets an alarmed look in her eyes and clinks her fork loudly against the side of her ceramic plate. Then she turns her head towards Dad and gives him an angry look without saying a word. It takes him a moment to understand why she's upset. Then he looks at me apologetically.

"I'm sorry, Julie," he says more calmly. "Jocelyn is your mother, and I worry about her...but I shouldn't have said that."

I feel a flash of my own guilt before it subsides.

"It's okay," I answer quietly.

I then excuse myself to go to the bathroom. Part of the reason is my overactive bladder, and the rest is to process this new info. How can I celebrate their pregnancy while I'm gonna end mine? Anyway, I've gotta deal with this queasiness before I try and eat anything.

Once I feel better, I let the smell of the dinner pull me back to the table. The rest of our conversation is light and uncontroversial. My sisters finish their food and ask for dessert, which is chocolate chip cookies. Maybe it's because of the chocolate bars I ate earlier, but the smell of the fresh baked cookies makes me slightly queasy again. I try to focus past it.

"The casserole was delicious, Bao," I tell her truthfully. "I love your cooking."

She grins bashfully. "Thank you so much."

"That's how she got my attention, too," Dad interjects, looking at me then her. "She catered one of our company events. I tasted the food and said to myself, I have *got* to see who made this! One look at this pretty lady, and she had me."

Bao blushes and struggles to maintain her smile. I'd be embarrassed, too. That's the start of what led to Mom divorcing him. While Dad focuses on putting more chicken casserole on his plate, Bao mouths the words "I'm sorry" to me. I quickly mouth "it's okay" back to her, shaking my head a little.

Dad met her the way I met Chet, except our positions were reversed. Like father, like daughter, I guess.

Bao gazes at the clock and says, "John, it's time for the girls to get ready for bed. Will you help them, please?"

He peers over to where Hua and Chow are watching TV in the living room and replies, "Oh, sure."

Once they've gone upstairs, Bao smiles again and looks at me with intrigue. "How are you doing, Julie?" she says, gently resting her hands against her stomach as she gazes at me.

She did not just do that!

"Your father told me what happened with your car getting towed," Bao continues, moving her hands to her lap. "Are you going to need rides anywhere?"

Like the abortion clinic? That's cringe. No, thanks.

"No, I'm good. It was more embarrassing than anything," I reply. "I should have found a better parking spot."

"You'd just left work. I'm sure you were tired," she soothes before smiling again.

This is Bao's gentle way of probing for information. I need to change the subject. "Was it hard for you to leave the workforce and be a stay-at-home mom?"

"It was a change at first," she admits. "But honestly, I feel more fulfilled being near my children."

"Great," I say, not sure what to do with that. "Um, to answer your earlier question, I'm...generally okay. My car getting towed was a shock, but Dad is going to help me get it back."

"Still, it was a tough time."

Tough time? Tough week? Tough month. Changing body. Sore breasts. Kid in my belly. Guilt over not telling Chet.

I have this sinking feeling as I realize Bao's been looking at me this whole time, studying me. I need to answer her. "Yeah."

"Want to talk about it?"

"Not really," I answer with a tired sigh. "But thanks."

Bao definitely knows I'm pregnant. She's probably got the same symptoms as me. But I still can't talk with *her* about it. She's everything I want Mom to be. But Mom is my mother, not her. I feel like turning to Bao would be one more betrayal, and I can't do that.

And it's not fair, because I really need a friend I can talk to. I know she'd understand. But I have to get through tomorrow.

"Thanks, Bao," I finally say. "I appreciate it."

•••

After Dad drops me off at home, I take my remaining munchies and head inside. Mom is sitting at the dining room table with her laptop, probably going over notes to prepare for another court case tomorrow. At least she allowed herself to change from her work clothes into a soft silk nightgown and robe.

"Why did your father drop you off?" she asks without looking at me. Then she answers my unspoken question. "I know the sound of his electric toy car."

"My car was towed," I say flatly, bracing for *Mom's Lessons in Why I'm a Failure, Volume Twenty-Seven*. "Dad gave me a ride."

"And took you to see his wife and your siblings," she adds nonchalantly. "I always know her perfume when I smell it." Mom has super senses. I'm over halfway across the room and she can pick up Bao's perfume. "And based on the time, you probably had dinner, too, right?"

"Right."

She finally looks up at me. I hate when she's in lawyer mode like this. "Let me guess, they made it some kind of occasion? Is there some tidbit of news you're probably reluctant to tell me?" Dang, she's good.

"Yes."

Her posture stiffens and she clenches her jaw. "Go ahead and tell me."

Yeah, that *really* makes me want to share information with you, Mom. "They're expecting."

Mom's facial expression stays the same, but her eyes are heartbroken. And I know why. She told me that, before she caught Dad cheating, they'd been trying to have another kid. She divorced him before that could happen. I sense her bitterness rise to the surface. "*Another* brat," she huffs, not caring how it sounds. "Well, he can afford it, I suppose. And his wife is young enough to crank `em out. Whatever."

I try to ignore her, but I can't. Maybe it's because I just spent time with them and maybe it's the pregnancy hormones. Or maybe I've heard this kind of garbage from Mom too many times. Whatever the reason, I snap, "Take that back, Mom!"

She looks genuinely surprised. "What did you say?"

"I know Bao was wrong to get with Dad when he was married to you," I shout, clenching my hands into fists at my sides. It feels good to get this out. "You were right to divorce him, but you don't have to keep punishing him or his new family!"

She stands up and takes a few steps towards me, studying me with narrowing eyes. "He doesn't need you to defend him."

"I'm not defending him, I'm defending myself!" I lash out. "I hear you curse Dad, his wife, or my *siblings* every single day! And at the same time, you ignore my life! And when you do notice me, it's to complain about how I'm doing everything *wrong!"* I step towards her now, shaking with adrenaline. "You spend more time mad at him than caring about me! You never comfort me. About anything!"

Mom is stunned silent. Good. Maybe she's listening. "We used to be so close...before the divorce! And now, we're not close at all! And Mom, I need you! I'm —" It almost slipped out. I purse my lips and look at her desperately. I'm starting to feel nauseous again. "I'm dealing with...more than you know. I really *need* you right now!" Tears slip down my cheeks and I shake my head. "But I won't ask for your help while you're still like this!"

Now I'm fighting sudden nausea as I turn and run to the bathroom. I slam the door shut before locking it. I fight the urge to vomit; that'll give away too much to Mom. But I get on my hands and knees in front of the toilet just in case, taking deep breaths to calm myself. I hear Mom's quick footsteps approaching. I'm so tired now. Tired, queasy, and hungry. Closing my eyes, I hear Mom talking but I can't understand her words. I want to go to my room to sleep but I'm still struggling with the nausea, hunger, and thoughts about the baby and tomorrow. After about five minutes, Mom stops talking and walks away.

I hope she's gone to her room. The queasiness has let up and I check my phone to distract myself. Chet called again. He left a voicemail and more text messages. Nothing I could say to him would make much sense right now. I drag myself to my feet, feeling unsteady as I move towards the kitchen. After warming up a plate of random leftovers from the fridge, I grab a lemon-lime soda and return to my room to eat. That helps me feel a lot better.

Great. I'm not tired anymore. And I still have this mess to deal with.

5

12:32 P.M. FRIDAY AUGUST 2nd – GZELLE COMPUTERS

My thoughts keep jumping between earlier this morning and now, starting with the alarm clock going off. I didn't sleep well. I couldn't stop thinking about the pregnancy and the abortion. I'm still torn. After I got out of bed, my feet were dragging so hard. I picked the first clothes I saw in the closet. I even forgot my car was gone when I went outside, so I had to book a PayMeRide to get to the office. Ever since then, I've been like a robot going through the motions, trying not to think about what I'm about to do. But as 1:30 gets closer and closer, I feel cornered. I have this sour, sinking feeling in my stomach. I should have told Chet by *now*. He deserves to know. But I can't! He can't know about this.

Right now, I'm waiting in front of the Gzelle building for another ride to take me to the Sanger Center where I'll get the abortion. Terminate the pregnancy. So many "nice" ways to describe what I'm really doing. I grip my hands into fists and swallow my anxiety. This early in the pregnancy and I'm already a failure as a mom. I never felt it move, haven't shown yet. The gray skies don't do anything to lift my mood. There's not even a breeze. It's like the calm before a storm. The app pings a notification: Carol is my driver and she's almost here. A minute later, I see her approaching in a big white SUV. I wave her down and she pulls alongside the curb.

The blonde with glasses rolls down the driver's side window. She reminds me of one of my college professors. At least she's in a good mood. Smiling, she says, "Julie?"

"That's me."

She points a thumb towards the back of the vehicle. "Hop in!" She's friendly, too. I can't place her accent, but it's definitely Southern. I open the back door and climb in.

She asks, "You're headin' to the Sanger Center, right?"

"Yes."

She nods and activates her left turn signal before re-entering the road. After a few seconds, we're on our way. "You mind if I gab a little, 'hon?"

"Go ahead," I say as I look out the window. Maybe it's the tint but everything looks drab. I feel so numb and tired right now, I just don't care.

"Can I ask you a personal question?"

"Sure, why not?"

"You're going to the Sanger Center. You don't have to tell me your business or nothin'," she begins in a compassionate tone. "But if you had a way — y'know, hypothetically speaking — to see the future and how things turned out, would you want to know?"

What a weird question. I thought she was gonna talk about the weather or something, not this. "What do you mean?"

She focuses ahead on the traffic as she continues. "You look kind of conflicted about your decision, and I can understand that. So, what I'm saying is, if you could know what happens, would you want that?"

"Well, sure! But no one can see the future..."

Exhaustion suddenly sweeps over me, and I can't seem to keep my eyes open.

•••

"We're here, 'hon!" Carol says brightly, startling me awake.

"I was napping?" I ask myself more than her. "I must have been too tired."

"Are you alright?" she asks. "Need any help getting out?"

"No, I'm okay," I say as I unbuckle the seatbelt and grab my purse. "Thanks."

The next few hours are surreal. There's payment and preparations. They give me a local sedative, and the procedure only takes ten minutes.

During my two-hour recovery in a small room on a bed, the sense of time seems to slow down around me. All I can do is think about what I've done, and I feel more alone than ever. I can't control the sudden heaving sobs that escape from me. There's a crushing weight on my chest from the regret. It gets worse after the anesthesia wears off, I put my clothes back on, and the nurse clears me to leave. I book a ride home with a different driver.

I'm not numb anymore. I know what I've done. I thought I'd feel free, but I don't feel that way at all. I...I feel like I'm shackled to a grave — my baby's grave — and now I'll never be free! I don't wanna call it murder...

When I get home, all I want to do is sleep. Mom is there. It looks like she's been waiting for me.

"Julie, are you alright?" she asks, her brow furrowing in concern. "You look terrible!"

I want to say something sarcastic, but I'm too tired. I just ignore her and start walking towards my room.

"Julie, can I talk to you about last night?" she asks sincerely. "I don't want to fight or criticize. I just want to talk, okay?"

Any other day, I'd be happy for the chance to have this conversation. But I'm out of my mind right now, and I'm about to collapse. I don't want anyone near me. "I don't feel good. I'm going to bed."

Mom puts her hand on my arm to get my attention, and I turn my head to look at her. "Julie, are you pregnant?"

Something breaks in my mind. I feel a smile spread on my face and I say, "No, I'm not pregnant." How fitting that I can actually tell her the truth.

She looks at me for several seconds and then says, "Well, whatever's bothering you, just know that you can talk to me about it, and I'll listen."

"Okay," I say, feeling my smile disappear. "Thanks."

Then I continue on to my room feeling all the warmth drain from me. I can tell I'm not who I was before the abortion. I fall onto my bed, hoping its softness will soothe my thoughts but no. I'm even more alone than before.

The phone rings and I see that it's Chet. I can't deal with him right now. I can't deal with him...I can't deal with him...

And I can't be his girlfriend anymore. He's not serious about us. And I won't see him as the man I should have spent my life with; I'll see him as the guy who got me pregnant. And it could happen again. I never could tell him about it, much less getting rid of it. How could I do that now?

None of this was right. None. None of it.

•••

I don't want to play see Dad. I don't want to go out. But here he is in the driveway ready to take me to get my car from the pound. It's past ten in the morning this Saturday and it's already hot. I barely notice the drive and I hardly say anything. Dad gives me concerned looks but doesn't pry. When we get there, I stand by him as he pays the cashier.

"Alright, Julie," Dad says. He looks worried. "Are you okay to drive?"

"I'll be fine, Dad," I say flatly. "Thanks for helping me."

All I do, week after week, is go to work and come home. I can't even play the piano. Mom keeps trying to suggest stuff to help me, but I'm not ready for anything. I'm completely not used to all this sudden attention from her anyway.

"Can I see Julie?" I hear Chet ask Mom at the front door. I'm in my room upstairs laying down on my bed with the door open. I'll let Mom talk to him. She'll say more than I would.

"I'm sorry, Chet, she's still not up for company," Mom replies softly.

"She won't answer my calls or texts, I'm very worried about her," he continues. "You know how many times I've come by. I even stopped by her job, but she won't see me." His voice becomes weak and dejected as he asks, "Has she broken up with me?"

"I...don't know," Mom answers.

It's a few seconds before he replies. "Alright," he says, sounding defeated. "Thanks, Ms. Greene. Goodbye."

Another week passes and Mom finally leaves me alone. She starts ordering delivery meals instead of cooking and spends most of her time in her room. That makes the house strangely quiet most of the time. It's the closest thing to peace I've had in this last month.

Chet doesn't call or text anymore. I delete his number from my contacts.

•••

Before I leave work, I stop by my desk to turn off my laptop and see that there's a memo or something on the keyboard. It reads, "Julie, this is an official write-up for your numerous unexcused absences over the last month. We have spoken about these absences twice now. If you accrue any more, it will result in your termination from this position. If you have any questions, you can discuss them with me." It's from my manager, Rachel. I'm not surprised. I shut down my laptop, close the lid, and lay the memo on top of it.

Then I grab my purse and stop by the restroom on the way out. Looking in the mirror, my breasts have almost returned to their original size. No more soreness or nausea. Without thinking, I put my hand to my stomach. I don't feel anything. Why should I? What I do notice is how tired I look, how poorly my blouse fits and how it doesn't match my skirt. My hair isn't much better. Whatever.

Once I get in my car, I just start to drive without a destination in mind. I don't want to go home and there's nowhere I really wanna be. I turn on the air conditioner and press a button on the radio to listen to a classical music station. I let the rhythm lead me as I pass neighborhoods and before long, I'm leaving the city limits. Cars are passing me by. I thought I was driving the speed limit, but I don't know. I just want to keep going, randomly choosing different highways to take. I want to be anywhere but home.

The colors of the twilight sky eventually blend into darker and darker shades. Headlights come and go. I heard my phone buzz a few notifications, and someone calls but I don't answer. The classical station has turned into static, and I didn't notice until now.

I look at my dashboard clock and see it's 10:45 pm. Then I see my gas is near empty. Feeling lightheaded, I pull over to the side of the highway and park.

Where am I?

My stomach hurts. I'm hungry!

What's going on? Why did I do this?

I put both hands on the steering wheel and look around eagerly. I didn't keep track of anything as I went and I'm a long way from anything familiar.

What am I doing?

These tears are burning on my face. I'm completely lost.

I don't have anything or anyone to hold onto.

I stopped talking to Dad, Bao, and my sisters because I didn't want to trouble them anymore. I dropped contact with my friends because fixing my mood doesn't equal fixing my problem. I let Chet go because of the baby. I cut Mom off because I don't want her sympathy; she had years to show that before now. And I'm probably gonna lose my job because I'm so depressed.

Why can't I reach out anymore?

There are birds chirping nearby. I listen to their songs, the beauty in their melodies. They're just animals, simple little creatures, but they have more peace than me.

I tried to fix everything by myself, and I ruined it all.

I need help to get out of this.

Where's my phone? Here it is. I'll check GPS and then call Dad. He'll know what to do.

Huh? The phone's off? I didn't turn it off.

Oh no! It's out of charge. Where's my charger cord? I thought it was in my purse. Did I leave it in my desk?

Oh crap! Oh no, okay, oh no — what do I do, oh my gosh —

•••

"We're here, `hon!" Carol says brightly, startling me awake.

What? Wait! I'm in the PayMeRide with Carol! She's right there. How? What time is it? The dashboard clock reads 1:22 P.M. Where's my phone? What? It has a charge? Friday, August 2nd? It's August 2nd!

I don't understand! Did I dream it all? The last entire *month* didn't happen??

Ahh! Sore breasts. I look down. They're still big. I'm...I'm still pregnant! My head is whirling in relief. Gazing down, I put my hands on my belly, and my tear drops land on my blouse. Baby! You're still here! This is real!

"Are you alright, miss?" Carol asks, looking at me through the rearview mirror.

Thank God! I still have a chance to fix all this! "Y-Yeah," I say nervously with a scratchy voice. "Gimme a minute."

She nods. "Alright. Take your time."

I look to the right out the window at the Sanger Center building and rage quickly fills my whole body. You people lied to me! You said the baby was just a clump of cells. You didn't warn me about the huge depression I could go through! I try to wipe my tears away, but they won't stop. Yeah, they lied to me. But they didn't isolate me from everyone. They didn't tell me to skip work or stop playing piano. They didn't break me inside. I did that. *I*...did that. I cup my hand over my mouth and feel nauseous.

I lean forward and say, "Carol, this may sound weird, but can you take me home instead? I've changed my mind."

She turns her head towards me and smiles. "That's not weird at all. It'd be my pleasure."

"Um, you can close out this ride and I'll book —"

"Don't worry about it," she assures me. "This one's on me. Just give me the address."

"Thanks."

6

1:46 P.M. FRIDAY AUGUST 2nd – JOCELYN GREEN RESIDENCE

My legs are wobbly as I get out of the SUV. I still don't understand this. What just happened to me?

I manage a weak wave at Carol as she drives off. After she turns the corner and is out of view, I start down the driveway to the house. Then I stop, deciding I want to give her a big tip. I mean, who would let their passenger sleep for however long in their car? I open the PayMeRide app and look at my history. What? Where is it? She was my most recent ride! The others are there, but this one isn't! I anxiously check my text notifications to see where I got charged. I remember that I did...but I can't find it now. I check my bank app and confirm it again. I never got charged.

Since I clearly got a ride, why's there no record of it anymore?

And it's not just the ride I took. It's the absence of the whole last month I thought I lived! I still can't make sense of this. Okay, let's go back before I got out of the SUV at the Sanger Center. Carol asked me about seeing the future: would I want to know what happened? And I did. I saw it all. Then I woke up and...it *didn't* happen?

Maybe I should just be glad it turned out this way instead. Yeah, I'm good with this. Gazing down, I stroke my belly with my hand. I'm definitely keeping you now.

And I've got to talk to Chet.

He doesn't answer when I call his number. He's probably at one of his jobs, so I leave him a voicemail. "Chet, it's Julie," I say nonchalantly. "Look, I'm not mad anymore, so let's just..." Wait, why am I still not being real with him? *Ugh*... "Chet, I'm sorry for getting upset and being out of touch so long. Will you give me a call back? I've been going through some stuff, and I'd like to explain. In person. Please call me back. Bye." No matter how he reacts, I'm telling him everything.

I'm so tired...and hungry! But I need to call Mom, too. I go inside and call her cell phone, but it goes to voicemail also, so I hang up. It's okay. I lock the door behind me and go to the kitchen. I feel like having something sweet and nutty, maybe with some pudding. I grab a spoon and bowl then fill it up. I start munching before I even get to the couch.

A minute later, my phone rings. Mom is calling me back already! I set the bowl down on the coffee table and answer, "Hi Mom, thanks for getting back to me!"

"Sorry I missed your call a few minutes ago," she says. "I was in a meeting."

The humble tone in her voice encourages me. Maybe she still wants to fix things. "It's okay," I tell her.

"Is everything alright?"

"I've gotta share something with you in person that's very important," I say honestly.

"After that meeting I just left, Cuddlebear, it'll be a pleasure to come home," she says.

Cuddlebear? My mind goes blank for a few seconds, and I blink twice. "Thanks, Mom. I love you!"

"I love you, too."

After hanging up, I hug one of the pillows, holding onto good memories from when she used to call me Cuddlebear years ago. Tears start to stream from my eyes. They're happy tears because things are starting to feel hopeful.

•••

Mom gets home a little sooner than she said. I'm at the piano playing Debussy's Arabesque No. 1 in E major. It's been a while since I've played, and this just feels right. I hear the front door close and Mom's heels clicking across the floor. "My word! I haven't heard you play anything like that before," she says. "It's beautiful!"

I let the last note I play linger before my foot lifts from the sustain pedal. Then I stand up and rush over to hug her. I need her to be the mom I knew as a girl again. And for the first time in forever, I feel like it's possible. My arms squeeze her tightly, and in my mind, I take back every mean thought I ever had about her.

"What's this?" she asks, sounding pleasantly surprised.

"Welcome home," I say gratefully.

"Are you feeling alright?" she wonders as she pulls back to look at me.

"I'm kind of moody," I admit, feeling my cheeks warm.

"Why are you moody?"

"I'm pregnant, Mom. And I've decided to keep the baby."

Her eyes go wide before they soften. "Thanks for confirming that. I'd been suspecting you were."

What? That's it? I stare at her. "That's it? Why didn't you say anything?"

She gives me this "what do you mean?" look. "Why didn't *you* say anything till now?"

My eyes sting as tears start flowing again. "I didn't think I could! I thought you'd tell me I was a failure again."

"A failure?" Mom repeats, sounding surprised. "I've *never* seen you as a failure!"

"Then why do you criticize all my life choices like where I work, how I look, and things I like?"

"I may have not agreed with some of your choices, but those weren't critiques of your character, Julie. I only wanted to guide you to success," she assures me. Then she sighs. "But if I made you feel like that...I am so sorry."

How long have I waited to hear her something like that?

Then Mom just hugs me. We just stay that way for a bit. It feels like someone taking a big weight off of me...from my heart.

I let go and look at her sincerely. "The baby is Chet's. I'm about three months pregnant," I tell her. "He doesn't know, but I'm going to tell him today."

"How long have you known?"

"A month," I tell her truthfully. "I planned to have an abortion. I even had an appointment set up for this afternoon, but I couldn't go through with it."

She winces, looking sad for me. Then she reaches out with both arms and says, "Aw, Julie, I'm glad you changed your mind." Pulling me close again, she adds, "Now that I know, I'll help you."

I almost collapse with relief. If I'd known she'd support me like this, I'd have done this weeks ago! It feels so good. *This* is my mom!

"Thanks," I say weakly. "I really need that."

Then Mom leads us to the dinner table.

"I wanted to talk to you, too," she says as she sits down, locking eyes with me. "I thought about what you said to me last night, and it was all true." Then she looks down, really sad. "I haven't let go of your father. I've been acting like John and I are still married, but we aren't. I haven't moved on like he did."

"Dad broke my heart, too," I say, shaking my head quickly. "And I haven't moved on, either."

"What do you mean?" she asks.

"I haven't told Chet about the baby yet because I was afraid he'd leave me. I...have rejection issues."

Mom sighs. "Oh, no, baby! I'm sorry we did that to you." She shakes her head and reaches over to put her hand on mine.

"You didn't know, Mom. I've kept too much to myself."

"I've been making a lot of mistakes...but I want things to get better between us," she says, now becoming misty-eyed. "I love you."

"I have, too, Mom, and I want the same thing. I love you, too," I tell her back. "I need you to be a part of my baby's life, too."

She's crying now, nodding. "Of course! It's our family. Oh, I can't believe my baby's having a baby! I hope you'll keep living here."

I give her an uncertain smile. "That'll depend on how Chet reacts when I tell him."

After she considers that a moment and nods, she says, "Fair enough."

•••

An hour later while I'm finishing the last of my granola yogurt in my bedroom, Chet calls me back. I stare at my phone in my shaking hand and take a calming breath. "Hey, Chet," I answer shakily. I was trying to sound relaxed, but it came across awkward.

"Julie, what's been going on with you?" he asks. "I accept your apology, but why did you ghost me like that?"

Ouch. "I need to see you so I can explain," I say nervously. "My car got towed yesterday and I can't get it back till tomorrow. Can you come get me?"

"Yeah, I can come get you," he says. "And Julie, be real with me."

"I will. I promise."

"Okay. I can be there in ten."

"Chet?"

"What is it?" He sounds defensive.

"I really am sorry for everything. And...I love you."

He's quiet for a second. "I'll see you soon."

"See you soon."

At least I finally said it out loud.

7

3:37 P.M. FRIDAY AUGUST 2nd – JOCELYN GREEN RESIDENCE

Less than ten minutes later, Chet texts me that he's here. I've changed out of my work dress into a light pink blouse and bluejeans. I check my hair in my bedroom mirror and fluff some life back into it. Looking down, I run my hand down my belly and realize how much of a curve there already is. I have a bump now! I go to my window and look through the blinds to see Chet's car next to the curb.

"He's here, Mom!" I say, calling across the house. "I'll be back later."

"Good luck," she calls back from her room.

I go downstairs, leave the house and quickly walk to his car. I hear the door unlock and sit down in the front passenger seat.

"So, what's going on?" he asks. "This isn't just about your car, right?"

"No," I reply with a shake of my head. "It's much more than that."

"Sounds serious. Is it about me? About us?"

"Yeah. Actually, it is." Here we go. "I'm pregnant."

His eyes narrow in confusion. "You are?" I nod. "How? We always used protection."

I shake my head again. "Not every time. Remember our vacation?"

His jaw drops. Then he squints and says, "You mean, that one time..?"

"That one time," I repeat, nodding slowly.

He looks lost, gazing around but not saying anything. Kinda the way I felt when I saw the pregnancy tests. Then he straightens up and focuses on me. Right at my belly. And I know he sees the bump.

I lay my hand on it as I say, "I've decided I'm keeping it. I mean, today, I almost had an abortion...but I couldn't go through with it." His face goes slack and there's instant hurt in his eyes.

"Why didn't you tell me as soon as you found out?!" he erupts.

"I was afraid."

He raises his eyebrows as he says, "Of what?"

"That you'd leave me over this! You wanted us to stay like we were, and we couldn't!"

He closes his eyes briefly and clenches his jaw. When he opens them again, he's angry. "So instead, you were gonna have an abortion and not tell me?!"

"I *didn't* do it, okay??" I shout back. "But I kept telling you I wanted more in our relationship! I talked about being soulmates and asked about our future, and you wouldn't commit! Why *wouldn't* I think about having an abortion? And why should I *tell* you? I was dealing with it all by myself anyway!"

He looks out the window, shaking his head in frustration. "You're my first serious girlfriend," he says in a low voice. "I guess I didn't want to mess it up, either. We've been having so much fun until recently." He sighs. "I thought if things moved too fast, I might scare you off. I didn't get what you were sayin' at all." Finally, he turns his head to face me again and says, "I'm not gonna leave you, Julie. I just need to think about what to do."

I frown. "What is there to think about? Besides, it's not just you. *We* need to think about what to do, right?"

He nods. "I've just never had a responsibility like this before."

I put both hands on my belly. "Do you think *I* have? I'm the one whose body is changing!"

"Yeah, I get that!" he replies, tapping nervously on the steering wheel. He's looking out the window again. "I need a day or two to think about this."

"A day or two," I huff. "Fine." I unlock the car door and get out.

"What are you doing?" he asks from inside the car. "You're leaving?"

I can't help it. My patience is gone, and I'm frustrated as I turn to him again. "Yes. Go ahead, take some time to 'deal with this.' Call me when you *really* want to talk."

"Julie, don't be like this," he says.

"You know what? I can't *help* being like this. It's the hormones," I blurt. Then I slam his car door and stomp back inside.

Mom is standing in the front doorway with her arms crossed as I approach. She moves out of the way to let me enter, then follows me inside. I turn towards her, ready for more of her sympathy. But that's not what I get.

"Did your little tantrum help you feel better?" she says, reminding me where I got my sarcasm from.

"I can't believe he acted like that! I did the right thing and told him the truth, but he just froze up and said he had to '*think about it*,'" I mock, fuming. "It's so...disappointing!"

"Julie, what did you expect?" she replies without her usual harshness. "Let's sit down and talk about this, okay?"

"Okay," I reply, following her to the couch.

"How old is Chet?" she wonders aloud as we sit down.

"Twenty-two."

"And you're twenty-five," she adds. "Now, think about this from his perspective for a moment. He's a young man working some part-time jobs, living on his own for the first time, and dating a beautiful girl a few years older than him. It hasn't been too serious, but you've been having a great time together."

I can't believe it. My mother the lawyer is advocating on my boyfriend's behalf?

"Today is different, though," she continues. "Today, you told him that you two are having a child together, you almost had an abortion, and you've been keeping all of this from him."

"Yeah, I know."

"Cuddlebear, you just shook up his whole world," she explains. "Did you think he'd just smile sweetly and propose on the spot?"

That would've been nice. Probably not realistic, but nice. "I didn't know what to expect."

"And neither did he," Mom says. "Now he has to make a choice."

"He already said he wasn't gonna leave me," I say.

Whoa. Chet said he *wasn't* gonna leave me! The thought of me having an abortion made him furious. I rest my hand on the bump again. Because it's his baby. And all I had to do was tell him about it.

"And you blew up at him?" Mom asks.

"Yeah. I...wasn't thinking," I say, embarrassed. "What do I do now?"

Mom stands up and takes a few seconds to look out through the blinds. "Why don't you ask him that?"

"What?"

"His car is still parked out front, Julie," she says hopefully. "Go talk to him again."

•••

I feel foolish walking down the driveway towards his car. I was pretty harsh before. I can see him from here. He looks deep in thought. It startles him when I knock on the passenger side window, but he immediately presses a button and lowers it.

"I'm sorry for blowing up at you," I say humbly. "I wasn't kidding about the hormones, but I shouldn't have done that. Can we talk some more?"

"Yeah, sure," he replies, sounding tired, before unlocking the car.

I sit back down and close the door. I'm gonna just shut up and let him talk this time.

He turns his head to look at me, and I can see something's already changed. He says, "This is pretty wild. You're having my kid."

"Yeah," I agree.

We look at each other and share that sense of uncertainty like we're gazing into the unknown together.

"We're not just boyfriend and girlfriend anymore," he adds.

"No, we're not."

Now he looks nervous. He turns his head away to the window then straight ahead before looking at me again. "I've been thinking about how to handle this." Mom was right. "I'm gonna find one steady job. Y'know, full-time work. And I'm gonna take care of you...and this baby...somehow."

I can't help but cry some more. Not from sadness. This is beautiful.

He reaches over and softly touches my cheek. "Julie, you're the first girl I've ever loved."

He loves me! He finally said it!

"Now, you tell me you're pregnant," he says. "At first, I was scared, then angry, but the more I think about it, the happier I get." He takes a breath and releases it. "My dad sometimes says life is all about change. And it's how we adapt to those changes that shows who we are."

"That's pretty deep."

"I wanna be the kind of man our kid will be proud of," he says tenderly. His eyes are sparkling as he gazes at me. "Julie, will you marry me?"

I don't even have to think about it. "Yes!"

•••

We go have some dinner nearby and talk some more before he takes me home. Mom and I watch the sunset from the chairs on the back porch.

"I feel so much relief now," I tell her. She gives me a very thoughtful expression. "What is it, Mom?"

"I'm glad you two are getting married," she admits. "But that means you'll be moving out, and that makes me a little sad."

I put my hand on hers. "It's not like we're gonna be moving into a house yet," I tell her. "We still have a lot to plan."

"I know. And you two will work this out," she replies reassuringly. "Chet's a good guy."

I nod. But something else is on my mind. "Mom, something really weird happened to me and I need to talk about it."

"Okay, go ahead," she answers. "I'll listen."

I tell her about that awful month that happened but didn't happen. She listens patiently though there are times when her eyes widen, or she looks at me with concern or confusion. I'd probably do the same if I were her.

"I can't explain what happened to you," Mom says. "It sounds like more than a dream, though." She gazes up into the night sky. "There's a whole universe out there that we barely understand." When I give her a confused look, she says, "Who am I to say what is or isn't possible? I was just remembering an old saying: 'When you have eliminated all which is impossible, then whatever remains, however improbable, must be the truth.'" Then she relaxes and smiles. "The important thing is that you and your baby are alright. I think you and Chet have a bright future ahead."

I return her smile and nod. "Thanks."

I repeat that quote in my head. I don't think I've ever heard it before. In this case, what is the truth here? Who was Carol? Was she just a kindhearted PayMeRide driver? Or was she an angel sent to give me a choice? I've got no other explanations. So is this that improbable truth? I'm not a spiritual person, but I do believe in God. And this seems like this was some kind of...I dunno, intervention? Whatever made things turn out this way, I'm grateful.

And I have a lot of questions.

EPILOGUE

Christmas is only a week away, and my due date is December 27th. Despite her busy work schedule, Mom's been taking time to do thoughtful things for me like making cinnamon-spiced herbal tea, raising the temperature to make it warm and cozy in the house, and lighting some vanilla-scented candles she placed on the countertops. All of it makes this finally feel like a home.

This evening, I've been looking through Chet's and my new Family Photo Album, a gift from our wedding in September. I look through this thing almost every day now. Mom bought me such a beautiful wedding dress and Chet looked so handsome in his tuxedo. It was the first time Mom allowed herself to be in the presence of Dad, Bao, and my sisters since the divorce was finalized. She behaved well for my sake. I turn the page and see Chet's parents, Wayne and Marsha. They're really nice people. They took the news about the baby pretty well and were supportive of our getting married. And there's my coworkers, Rachel and Suzie. I turn to the next page, where Chet and I faced one another and took our vows. Pastor Greenwood looks so proud of us.

"When's Chet getting back from work?" Mom asks from the kitchen, interrupting my memories. She's making snickerdoodle cookies — my favorite! Just the scent alone is amazing.

Looking at my phone, I see it's 6:32 p.m. "He should be home a little after eight."

After Chet and I got married, Mom welcomed us to stay with her, so she could support us through the rest of my pregnancy. She even let us have her room. She says she likes my room better, that it stirs up a lot of good memories. We don't want to depend on her good will indefinitely but it helps a lot right now.

"If I go to bed before he gets home, let him know there's plenty of leftovers in the fridge," she says.

"I will."

"Does he still like working at the catering company?" she wonders as she walks over, munching on a cookie with her own mug of tea in the other hand.

"It seems like it," I answer honestly, but I can't help pouting some. "But it also takes him away from me, and he needs to be here, too."

Mom quickly slides the mug onto the coffee table in front of us and snuggles in next to me. "He'll be here soon. You'll live."

"I don't have to like it," I mutter.

Mom's wearing sage and white sweats, her hair's pulled back into a messy bun, and I think she has a brighter maternal glow than me. Smiling, she puts her arm around me, glances at my abundant belly, and asks, "Are you both doing better than earlier?"

"Yes," I say with relief. "I mean, he was fine. I had some heartburn. But I'm better." Almost on cue, the baby shifts and starts stretching upward against my stomach. "Now, he's doing pushups," I laugh.

"He hears us talking," Mom asserts with a grin. "Maybe he wants to join the conversation."

I love seeing Mom like this. The hardness is gone. This pregnancy has given us so many ways to get closer. She's opened up, telling me new stories about being pregnant with me and my early years.

"Or maybe he's telling us to shut up," I joke.

"Maybe," she laughs. And it just does something to my heart. Then she asks, "So, have you and Chet decided on his name?"

I nod and place a hand softly on my belly. "Victor David Morgan."

Mom looks impressed. "I like it! How did you come up with Victor?"

I look at my belly again, this time with mixed feelings. "I wasn't sure if I wanted him at first," I answer. "And I came so close to —" I can't finish that sentence. "But I kept him, and he's almost here. It's like a victory...so, he's Victor."

Mom nods. "I can't argue with that, Julie. It's beautiful."

We hear the tingling keys notification from my phone. Reading the text excites me and I say, "It's from Dad! Bao's gone into labor. They're heading to the hospital."

Mom surprises me by grabbing her mobile phone from the coffee table and dialing a number. A couple of seconds later, I hear a click as someone answers. "John, it's me," she begins. "Julie told me about Bao. You can drop the girls off here so you can be there for your wife." She listens to his reply, then adds. "Of course, it's fine, or I wouldn't have offered. Drive safely, and we'll see you in a few minutes. Bye."

"I did not expect that," I say with some amusement.

"Your sisters showed impeccable behavior at the wedding," she deflects. "And I have to admit, they are pretty adorable."

"And maybe things are just a little better between you and Dad?" I ask.

"He'll have enough to deal with in the delivery without having to keep up with small children," she says in a guarded tone. "They can stay here for a few hours."

"Thanks, Mom."

Dad arrives ten minutes later, ringing the doorbell. Mom answers because I'm not moving if I don't have to. But I've got a good view of the door from here. Despite his good-natured smile, I can see that Dad's stressed, but the girls are happy.

"Hi, Julie's mom!" Hua says cheerily.

"Hi, Julie's mom!" Chow echoes. "Where's Julie?"

Mom can't help but giggle a little. "Hello, Hua and Chow," she says pleasantly. "It's good to see you again." Then she points in my direction. "Julie's in the living room."

"Thanks, Julie's mom!" they both say as they rush towards me.

I make myself stand up and turn to the right, so I can hug them. "C'mere, munchkins!"

When they step back a second later, they both look at me as I knew they would.

"Wow, Julie! I think you're bigger than Mom!" Hua says in amazement.

"She *is* bigger than Mom!" Chow adds, intrigued. "Can we touch your tummy?"

If those words came from anyone but these two, I'd be insulted. But they're four and eight; they don't know what tact is. And they're not exactly wrong. My pride will recover. "Yes," I reply. "Just be gentle, okay?"

"Is the baby a boy or a girl?" Hua asks, captivated as she lightly strokes my belly.

"It's a boy," I confirm. These little girls are gonna be aunts at very young ages.

"Mom's having a girl!" Chow blurts as she puts her hands on either side of my stomach. Then she looks up at me and adds, "We get another little sister."

I smile and nod at her. "Yes. And you get a boy nephew."

"What's a neffew?" Chow asks.

As we continue our conversation, I gaze over at Mom and Dad and hear them talking.

"I really appreciate this, Jocelyn," he says gratefully. "Bao asked me to give you her thanks, too."

"You're welcome," she replies. Then she points towards the door. "Now take your wife to the hospital before she gives birth in your car." I can hear a little humor in her voice. Wow.

He nods. "Alright," he says. Then he looks at me. "Everything okay, Julie?"

I wave and say, "Everything's fine, Dad. Text or call when she's had the baby, okay?"

"Will do." He waves at my sisters. "Bye, girls!"

They both wave and say, "Bye, Daddy!"

An hour later, the door unlocks, and Chet comes in. I'm still getting used to the sight of him in his blue and gray catering uniform.

He starts to open his mouth, but I shush him from across the room. When he looks at me funny, I softly say, "My sisters are upstairs in Mom's room." Then I lumber forward and give him a hug. "Welcome home, babe!"

He gives me a kiss, then quietly asks, "Why are your sisters here? Is everything okay?"

"Bao's in labor, so Mom told Dad to bring the girls here."

Mom lays down on the couch. "Well, now that Chet's home, I'm going to get some sleep, too."

"How are you and Victor doing?" Chet asks as we ascend the stairs to go to our room.

"We're doing fine," I reply with a very tired smile. "He just keeps moving around all the time."

"Isn't that normal in the ninth month?"

I look at him with furrowed brows. "Yes, Chet," I say sarcastically. "It *is* normal. That doesn't make it fun."

"Oh. Right. Anything I can do to help you feel better?"

That brings my smile back. "Just spend time with me. I've missed you."

"I've missed you, too."

"And maybe order me some food."

"Okay."

"Massage my shoulders?"

"Sure."

"Thanks, Babe."

•••

Twenty-two hours of labor. That's how long it took to bring our son into the world. But now, I finally get to meet this little boy. He cries with perfectly healthy lungs, and I can see he has a full head of dark brown hair. The nurses work with him for a few minutes, cleaning him off, taking his measurements until they bring him to me wrapped in a little blue blanket. Chet is at my side.

"Julie, he's beautiful!" he says breathlessly.

"Uh-huh" is all I can manage to say. I can't take my eyes off of our son as the nurse places him on my chest.

Victor is a marvel to me. Twenty-one inches long, he weighs eight and a half pounds.

And he was born on Saturday, December 28th at exactly 1:30 P.M.

Allen Steadham created comic books and webcomics before he started writing novels. He has been married to his wife, Angel, since 1995 and they have two sons and a daughter. When not writing stories, Allen and his wife are singers, songwriters and musicians. They have been in a Christian band together since 1997. They live in Central Texas. You can learn more about Allen Steadham, his books, upcoming endeavors, follow his blog, and subscribe to his newsletter at **https://allensteadham.com**

Thank you for your interest in *Choosing Life: A Pro-Life Anthology*.
All proceeds from the sale of this anthology will be donated
to pro-life non-profits organizations.

www.ingramcontent.com/pod-product-compliance
Lightning Source LLC
LaVergne TN
LVHW090603110826
845146LV00001B/248